P9-EKY-133

PROJECT Sunlight

I am Jared, citizen of the universe, member of the Celestial Penmen.

I decided yesterday that I shall concentrate my study upon the first person to round the corner of Ridge and Genesee in the city of Rochester after 6:00 PM today. That moment even now approaches, and I am filled with anticipation. This residential street is not busy at the moment as most of the working class have already made their way home. The clock on the Midtown Bank says 5:56. I fasten my eyes upon the designated corner. Leaves swirl about the buildings in a brisk fall wind. They remind me that it must be very frightening to live on a planet where, sooner or later, everything dies.

A boy races around the corner, tennis racket in hand, but it is only 5:59. I am almost sorry. He's a fine-looking lad.

Now. Right now. The very next person. It is 6:02. Soon it will be dark, and few will venture out, for the city streets of Planet Earth are not safe at night.

But wait. A small figure rounds the corner, her belted coat whipping in the wind. A young woman. Or maybe not so young. Thirtyish I'd say. Funny, I'd never thought of studying a woman. They seem rather complex creatures. She, lithe and quick in movement, is now backlighted with the late October sun's thin silver rays. Suddenly I know what I will call her: *Sunlight.* Of course. It is perfect.

PROJECT *Sunlight*

by
JUNE STRONG

Southern Publishing Association, Nashville, Tennessee

Copyright © 1980 by
Southern Publishing Association

This book was
Edited by Gerald Wheeler
Designed by Dean Tucker
Cover painting by Bill Myers

Type set: 10/12 Souvenir
Printed in U.S.A.

Library of Congress Cataloging in Publication Data

Strong, June.
   Project Sunlight.

                                                        I.   Title.
PZ4.S918463Pr   [PS3569.T713]   813'.54   80-13011
ISBN 0-8127-0289-1

Acknowledgments

A special thank you to Rob and Jacquie, Kent and Billie-Jean, Steph and Nina, who cared and counseled.

For Nina

Contents

Preface

The story upon these pages is a dramatization of the final events that await our planet, and the young woman, Sunlight, simply a composite of us all. She represents our need of the Prince, a need that we must recognize and meet before we can be whole.

For the sake of the story I have taken an occasional liberty. Let the reader remember that God alone knows the details, and they are not necessary to our salvation. The real issue is not *how* He will come, or even *when,* but only whether or not you and I will be ready.

"We are made a spectacle unto the world, and to angels, and to men" (1 Corinthians 4:9).

Cast of Characters

JARED	an angel
SUNLIGHT (Meg)	a young divorcée
MICHAEL	Sunlight's friend from childhood
JENNY AND CAROL	Sunlight's children
JIM	Sunlight's former husband
MARIE	Jim's present wife
SYBIL	Sunlight's neighbor and friend
BILL	Sybil's husband
JOE	young pastor friend of Michael's
JEAN	Joe's wife
JASON AND TAMMIE	Joe and Jean's children
DALE, ANNE, ROY, ELLEN, MR. LAIRD	members of Joe's congregation
KELLY	work associate of Sunlight's
STATE POLICE	

Chapter One

I am Jared, citizen of the universe, member of the Celestial Penmen. At the moment my gaze is riveted upon the corner of Ridge and Genesee streets in the city of Rochester, New York. While I am waiting, I will tell you why this particular spot on a tiny, faraway planet is so important to me. It is the sober assignment of the Celestial Penmen to chronicle the activities of Planet Earth. We have recorded wars and treaties of peace, floods, famines, revolutions, eras of prosperity, and atrocities beyond our sanctified imaginings. The church, of course, has been the focal point of our observations, the Prince having invested in it far more than it can ever comprehend.

An old man just rounded the corner. A shabby, soiled old man who long ago bruised the fragile, shimmering gift of life in grimy, careless hands. But the time is not yet. I am relieved.

We, the Celestial Penmen, have been amazed at the shortsightedness of humans. They buzz about as if the earth were the center of the universe instead of just a speck in the cosmic dust. Mankind has little conception of its plight, though the King has spelled it out for them in the book they call the Bible. Many don't take it seriously, some don't believe it at all, and even those who profess to follow the Prince often seem more excited about a new car or a church social than about His return. He *does have* a few committed ones, though, and they bring Him such joy. Sometimes He's positively radiant watching one here or there who's consistently

15

His person.

I used to feel a holy impatience with them all, for His sake. Their ingratitude seemed unpardonable. Such an arrogant race with so little to be arrogant about. But slowly, over the centuries I've come to love them, especially since He went to live with them. Watching Him out there, so much one of them sometimes I had to take a second glance to pick Him out of the crowd, I began to see them through His eyes. When I saw His weariness, I understood theirs. When the Rebel pursued Him relentlessly, I conceived the hoplessness of their condition. When *He* wept, I felt their tears. So it has been with a dawning compassion that I've recorded the activities of earthlings over the past two thousand years.

> A couple comes into view, a handsome couple in the prime
> of earth-life. She is holding his arm, and they are laughing.
> Now what would I do with a couple when I am looking for
> only one? Fortunately there are a few moments left.

So let's get on with my explanation. Of late I have grown weary of observing the masses, of transcribing their whimsical loyalties to one corrupt leader after another. My heart has bled for starving millions and trembled for the frolicking, indifferent rich. I have found myself with a persistent desire to concentrate upon individuals, though that is the direct assignment of the Recording Angels, a completely separate segment of the Celestial Penmen.

So obsessed did I become with the idea that I sought permission from the King Himself to concentrate my attention upon one earthling. I made it clear that I did not desire to record the individual's every thought and motive with the precise accuracy required for the judgment but simply to compile a more general observation of one human's reaction to the sin environment. He granted me permission, and I am more excited than I have been in centuries, though I cannot decide just why.

I've had many suggestions from my fellow penmen, who graciously share my excitement. Some have urged I choose a newborn baby, others recommend a youth of superior intelligence. I myself considered searching for a child of strong spiritual bent, but at last I decided that I did not want any such controls upon my experiment. I shall pick someone at random.

In fact, I decided yesterday (you will note I am already using the time terminology of earth) that I shall concentrate my study upon the first person to round the corner of Ridge and Genesee in the city of Rochester after 6:00 PM today. That moment even now approaches, and I am filled with anticipation, for my study shall center about this particular citizen of earth, whoever it may be, as long as his life shall last. This residential street is not busy at the moment, most of the working class having already made their way home. The clock on the Midtown Bank says 5:56. I fasten my eyes upon the designated corner. Leaves swirl about the buildings in a brisk fall wind. They remind me that it must be very frightening to live on a planet where, sooner or later, everything dies.

A boy races around the corner, tennis racket in hand, but it is only 5:59. I am almost sorry. He's a fine-looking lad.

Now. Right now. The very next person. It is 6:02. Soon it will be dark, and few will venture out, for the city streets of Planet Earth are not safe at night.

But wait. A small figure rounds the corner, her belted coat whipping in the wind. A young woman. Or maybe not so young. Thirtyish I'd say. Funny, I'd never thought of studying a woman. They seem rather complex creatures. She, lithe and quick in movement, is now backlighted with the late October sun's thin silver rays. Suddenly I know what I will call her: *Sunlight.* Of course. It is perfect.

I watch her hurry down the street, mount the steps of an

apartment complex, and take an elevator to the seventh floor. She seems nervous in the elevator, I note, as though she cannot tolerate delay. Finally she enters an apartment on which the name plate reads MEG ADAMS and greets two small girls, one perhaps nine or ten, the other about six. For a moment, while she's hugging them, her face softens, but she tosses her coat onto the back of a chair and her entire being is once more tuned to the pace of city earthlings.

The older child—Sunlight calls her Jennifer—has hamburgers already sizzling in an electric skillet, and the little one is setting the table. Sunlight puts a tossed salad together, and they sit down to eat. I eavesdrop shamelessly, for I wish to learn everything about my new project as quickly as possible.

Sunlight: I worry about your using the electric frypan, Jen. You must be supercareful. Promise me.

Jenny: I won't get burned, Mom. Don't forget I'll be ten in two weeks.

Sunlight: Promise me, Jen!

Jenny (annoyed): OK, OK. I promise I'll be careful. I wish you'd tell Carol not to eat Twinkies before supper. See, now she's just picking at her food.

Sunlight: Your sister's right, Button. Absolutely no sweets before supper.

Carol: Tell her to get off my back. She's not my boss just because she's three years older.

Jenny: Oh, yes I am when Mom's not around.

Sunlight (impatient now): That's enough, you two. After hassling customers at the store all day, I can't take your squabbling when I get home. My nerves are shot. Now shut up.

(The two girls eat quietly, silver and china fighting off the silence with businesslike sounds. Sunlight leaves her meal half eaten and moves to the couch to watch

the news on television.)

Carol: Daddy called to say he won't stop by for us on Saturday. He's going to be out of town.

Sunlight: Don't talk to me about your father. He hasn't been here for weeks. Why does he bother to call with those phony excuses? Hey, Baby, don't look like that. He's not worth a single, tiny tear.

(They tidy the kitchen and watch Happy Days *before Sunlight sends the girls off to bed. She sits, then, in the dimly lit room, the smoke of a cigarette wreathing her small, well-shaped head. Her face in the shadows is pretty, yet somehow old and sad.)*

I feel an anger as I watch her. An anger at the Rebel, and what earthlings have endured at his hands. I long to write across the sky the simple solution to their predicament.

Jesus Christ, Prince of the Universe, is *yours,* Planet Earth. Yours to heal your sickness, comfort your loneliness, and make you whole again. Lift up your heads. Laugh and dance and sing. Take the gift He's bought for you at such cost, and give Him your love in return.

But I know, even as I compose my celestial bulletin (*i*'s all dotted with stars) that men would barely lift their eyes to read, nor would they believe. They've seen *Star Wars* and *Close Encounters of the Third Kind* and *Black Hole,* so what else is new?

Sunlight stubs her cigarette in the ashtray and dozes in her chair. Only a streetlight nudges the darkness about her. A darkness deeper than she knows. I look across the Holy City to the throne, where the Prince and His Father can be seen together. There is light aplenty there. Light enough to turn puny earth into a blazing sun. But it's not light that humans need so much as love. If they only knew that the Prince bathes their small sphere constantly in His love. I see the same loneliness in *His* eyes as He observes them that I saw in Sunlight's tonight, and I begin to understand a little of His sorrow. They need each other, those earthlings and the Prince. They are bound together in some mysterious way beyond my understanding. Maybe it happened at the cross—or maybe before, in the stable at Bethlehem or just when He walked their roads, ate at their tables, and touched their sick.

Strangely, He is no less ours because He is theirs. But they are infinitely more ours because they are His. And on that confusing observation I close my journal for the night.

One week has passed, and I know a great deal more about Sunlight than when I closed this journal last Tuesday. She works in cosmetics at Sibley's downtown store, looking very chic and professional as do most of her fellow workers there. Conscientious, she gives each customer courteous attention, yet an anger festers within. Her conversation with her fellow workers is witty and intelligent but often cynical.

She is shattered at the very core of her being, as are many earthlings, but she functions on the residues of that magnificent resiliency with which the Prince endowed man at the beginning. Sunlight forces her doubts and fears into the far corners of her mind, where, unfortunately, they smolder.

Sometimes irritation even tinges her love for her children because she has to be both mother and father to them. She envies what she interprets as their carefree existence. They aren't, of course, carefree. The bitterness between their parents has washed over them until already their spontaneity has succumbed to a puzzled, painful acceptance of life. I am beginning to realize that my journal cannot be the simple telling of Sunlight's story, for so interwoven are earthlings' lives, I shall find myself, of necessity, including others in my study, but only as I must to record every facet of Sunlight's experience.

It pains me when she is harsh with the children. They seem so defenseless, though the little one is strong-willed and stands her ground.

If only I could connect Sunlight with the Prince. That, however, is Earth Friend's work and, though His presence is ever about her, she senses no need of His help. It is frustrating to be limited to watching. I have new respect for the work of the Recording Angels. What sadness they must have endured over the years as they've watched millions of individuals live out their days with no interest in Heaven's concern for them, only to die fearful and alone. But that *must not* be Sunlight's fate. Followers of the Prince dwell all over her city. Surely one of them will seek her out and tell her of Him.

It is Saturday night. For some reason earthlings experience a kind of madness on Saturday night. Even the most docile of them go out to eat or settle about the television in their homes with bowls of popcorn. But the restless ones. Ah, me! What they don't resort to to quiet their loneliness! The cities teem with ugliness. Sunlight is disco dancing with her friend, a young man she has known since childhood. A rather decent young man, all things considered. He takes her dancing and tries to fill the gaps in her life with his friendship. I watch them now, as best I can through the smoky haze. She is like an autumn leaf in her swirling red dress, her cheeks flushed with excitement. Both she and her friend, whom she calls Michael, are caught up in the frenzy of the dance, an almost hypnotic blend of light and sound and movement, far removed from the Peaceful Land in which I dwell. Sometimes, on Saturday nights, I despair that men will ever find the Prince . . . that when He returns to bring them home He will discover that no one awaits Him. But, of course, that will not happen. I am only discouraged because it sometimes seems that Planet Earth is ablaze with its own destruction.

Later, in the car, they talk, Sunlight and Michael. The flush of excitement has subsided, and she is pale and tired, almost as though her soft red dress is consuming her delicacy, like flames nibbling at a paper flower.

Sunlight: How come we had to leave early? I'd like to dance forever.

Michael: Why?

Sunlight: Because when I'm dancing, especially if I've had a few drinks, I can forget. I don't worry about the girls. I don't think about Jim. I don't remember all those picky, middle-class matrons at the store. I forget how eerie the apartment gets after the girls go to bed at night. I forget how afraid I am of all the years ahead. What if I get sick and can't pay the rent? What if the girls become wild teenagers and I can't handle them? What if I can never love anyone again? Or no one ever loves me? See why I like to dance, Michael?

Michael: You know that I won't let anything happen to you.

Sunlight: I suppose you're going to stay single all your life just in case I stub my toe. *(She laughs wryly.)*

Michael *(smiling):*   I'll be here tomorrow and the next day. Isn't that good enough for now?

Sunlight: I see the years just unrolling ahead of me, dull and empty. *(Her cigarette glows red in the darkness.)* And then death. I'm scared of death, Michael. Even more scared than I am of life.

Michael: Those are long thoughts for a young woman, Maggie. You need your rest. That's why I brought you home early tonight. When you get up tomorrow, you'll find Death will keep his distance.

Sunlight: Huh! Sometimes he walks to work with me. But—forget it! Thanks for everything. Next Saturday night get yourself a carefree chick who's not wallowing in self-pity. If it weren't so ironic, coming from me, I'd even go so far as to suggest that you get married.

Michael *(thoughtfully):*   I've considered it.

   (He walks her to the door of her apartment, promises to call, and drives the baby-sitter home. Sunlight turns out the lights, gets into her robe, and sits a long time looking out across the lighted city. The ashtray is full when she finally draws the drapes and goes to bed.)

I have wondered much about Sunlight's ex-husband. Today he came to take the girls on an outing. Overjoyed, they threw themselves into his arms with an enthusiasm I had not seen in them before. I decided he could not be all bad. In fact, I have yet to discover an earthling who is *all* bad. A short, athletic-appearing young man, he was a little uneasy in his visitor's role. He made light chitchat with the children as they slipped into their coats, even trying to draw Sunlight into the conversation, but she would have none of it. Sometimes I think I chose a most inappropriate name for her, but she does have reason to be hurt, and her hurt erupts as fierce hostility. After he had gone, she flew into a fit of housecleaning where none was really needed. A tidy housekeeper, she has little upon which to vent her frustrations in time of need. I noted, as she scoured the bathroom tile, that tears ran down her cheeks, though she made not a sound.

Now he has brought them home, his daughters, disheveled and rosy from a canoe trip on the Genesee River. A young woman, whom I assume is his new wife, waits outside in the car. I'm sure he can tell Sunlight has been crying, though she barely acknowledges his presence. Jennifer and

Carol bubble over with the adventures of the day, but Sunlight shoos them off to the tub. Jim attempts to break through her defense.

Jim: Can't we be friends, Meg, at least for the sake of the girls?

Sunlight: Your concern amazes me. You haven't seen them in a month.

Jim: It's not always easy. Marie often makes plans for the weekends in which two little girls just don't fit.

Sunlight: I'll bet she does!

Jim: Other people get divorces and go on being friends. Why must you be so difficult? I know the alimony's not a lot, but it's the best I can do at the moment. I didn't set out to fall in love with someone else. It just happened. I'm sorry, Meg. I really am. I've told you that a hundred times.

Sunlight: Please go, Jim. You can come for the kids any time, but don't ask me to listen to your theatrics afterward. And don't keep Cinderella waiting. She might turn into a pumpkin, or whatever.

Jim *(grinning):*   I still like your wit, even when it's sticking in my back. Good-night, Meg.

The Prince came by just now and asked me how I was getting along with my special project. When I told Him, He smiled and was quiet for a moment. Then He said, "So you call her Sunlight. That is good. Write your story well, Jared, and in the writing you will learn much." Now what did He mean by that?

But He knew her instantly by my description. He knows each earthling as if there were no other. I fear the joys of this land will mean nothing to Him until He brings them home.

Chapter Two

A strange thing happened today. I had been casting my eye over the Christian community, hoping someone would seek out Sunlight, but there isn't much seeking going on. Lots of activity in some churches, utter stagnation in others, but not a great deal of concern for those who don't know the Prince. Earth Friend, however, works with what He has. Sunlight was going up in the elevator with a nice-looking middle-aged woman whom I'd seen in the building before.

Woman: Aren't you my neighbor in 721?

Sunlight: Well, yes, I guess I am, though I must admit I don't know a soul in the building. When you work you know . . . My name's Meg, Meg Adams. I'm glad to know you.

Woman: I'm Sybil Norris, Meg, and I have a confession to make too. I've been keeping my eye out for someone in this building who is alone. Sometimes I get so bored and fed up with everything that I wish for one of those gas stoves. . . . It's awful to get out of bed in the morning and not have a thing to look forward to.

Sunlight: Is your husband dead?

Sybil: No, he's very much alive. Alive and prosperous and too busy piling up money to even wonder what I do with myself all day. Most of the time he's traveling, and he thinks as long as he keeps my checking account current that he has fulfilled his obligation. So I sit around thinking up new ways to spend money.

(Elevator reaches their floor, and they walk down

the hall together.)

Sunlight: Well, I'm alone a lot, too, but I guess that's about the extent of our mutual problems. I spend a lot of *my* spare time figuring out how to make ends meet.

Sybil: That would at least be a challenge, though no doubt an unnerving one at times.

(They reach Sunlight's door.)

Sunlight *(casually, not really meaning it):* I've enjoyed meeting you. Maybe we could get together for coffee sometime.

Sybil: I'd love that. In fact, why don't you run down to my end of the hall tonight after you get the children to bed? I'm in the suite at the end.

Sunlight: I always wondered who the lucky lady was who lived there. But I don't like to leave the children alone, even just to go down the hall, so why don't you come to my place? It's certainly no luxury suite, but I make good coffee.

Sybil: Hey, I'm looking forward to it already. What time?

Sunlight: The kids should be settled down by 9:00. See you then.

I knew by the way Sunlight set about picking up things in the apartment she was a little impatient with what she had gotten herself into, but somehow I have a good feeling about this new friendship. Sybil has an openness and honesty that I like.

(Jenny and Carol are lying on the living-room rug, watching reruns of the Flintstones.*)*

Sunlight: We have to fix a quick supper and get this place straightened up. I'm having a friend over after you girls go to bed.

Carol: Is it Michael? We want to see him too.

Sunlight: No, it's not Michael. It's just the lady who lives in that big apartment down at the end of the hall. Met her in the elevator. You can say hello to her if you get into bed pronto afterward. Jen, help me with supper, and Carol, pick up all the junk around on the floors.

Jenny *(quietly):* I'm not doing very well in school, Mom.

Sunlight: What do you mean you're not doing well in school? You've always been a top student.

Jenny: I can't seem to concentrate anymore. My mind just wanders around. Mrs. Morrison scolded me today. She said it was just plain carelessness for me to get 65 on a math test.

Sunlight: Jen, what happened? *Are* you getting careless?

Jenny: I don't know, Mom. I look at the tests, and I just don't know the answers like I used to. Sometimes when Mrs. Morrison is talking, I realize all of a sudden I haven't heard a word she's said for five minutes.

Sunlight: Well, you better start listening, young lady. Maybe I need to have a talk with Mrs. Morrison. Now, let's eat.

Carol *(a forkful of macaroni and cheese poised midair):* I'm glad Jen's not hauling *A*'s anymore. Now my report cards won't look so bad beside hers.

Sunlight: Just eat, will you? Your father expects both of you to keep your grades up. I think you're watching too much television. All those old movies after school aren't meant for kids.

When Sybil comes, the girls, in nightgowns and still moist from the tub, appraise her silently. Carol is tiny and dark like her parents, but Jennifer must resemble some more distant ancestor, for she's tall for her age and with hair the color of ripe wheat. Sybil's response to them is warm but low-key. After Carol kisses her mother good-night, she goes to Sybil, pixie face upturned, and asks, "You want one too?" She's always the more outgoing of the children, with a lovable elfin quality.

Jennifer runs deep and is not handling her parents' separation well. She says good-night politely and goes off to bed with no display of affection. Sybil and Sunlight chat about superficial matters, then Sunlight talks about her marriage.

Sunlight: Jim and I were married young. Too young, I suppose. The spring I graduated from high school. He was two years ahead of me and well into college. We'd been high school sweethearts, and somehow our romance survived the separation. There'd been times when I'd been tempted to date when he was gone, and I'm sure those swinging college girls must have been a temptation to him, too, but we were really in love and the weekends he came home made the waiting all worthwhile.

The first years of our marriage were perfect. I worked so he could finish school. Because there was no money, we lived simply. When Jim graduated and Jenny was born, we thought the struggle was all behind and only joy ahead. Jim was hired as a science teacher in the same suburban high school where he's teaching now. Eventually we bought a house, and Carol was born. Everything was ordinary but wonderful. I thought it would always be like that. We'd work to get the girls through college, become useful in the community, and grow old together. And it was that way for eight years.

Then one night, after the girls were in bed and Jim was wiping the dishes for me, he said, "Meg, I've fallen in love with someone else." Just like that. That's when my life ended. Even now I can still feel the warm coziness of the kitchen, see him standing there with the dish towel in one hand and a dinner plate in the other. I tried to fit what he was saying into the surroundings, and I thought I was losing my mind. Numbly I waited for him to laugh and tell me it was a joke, but I saw pity in his eyes—pity for me—and I knew he was not playing games.

The girl he'd met was the art teacher at the high school. They had been thrown together a lot in various school activities, and he hinted that her world was a bit larger than mine . . . her interests broader. Just the old soap opera of the high school sweetheart who puts her man through college and then loses him because she's more interested in wallpapering the living room than discussing the nation's economy. So, the girls and I have been without him for nearly two years, and I should be used to it, but I guess I never will be.

Sybil: So you lost your husband to another woman and I've lost mine to work, which leaves us both alone. Even when Bill's home, he's so buried in the *Wall Street Journal* that he might as well be gone. The only time he's ever excited or happy is when the price of gold goes up.

Sunlight: At least I have the girls. That helps a lot, though I'm so tired and irritable all the time that I've turned into a wretched mother. Jen's grades are going downhill, and I fear she's all knotted up inside. Probably needs counseling, but psychiatrists definitely aren't in my budget.

Sybil: Speaking of being all knotted up inside, a couple of weeks ago I got so lonely I went to an evening meeting in that little church down the street. Once or twice in the late summer the door had been open as I'd walked by, and their singing sounded warm and inviting, so I thought it might be better than staring out the window of my apartment another long night. They welcomed me like a long-lost friend, and I *did* enjoy the singing, but to be perfectly honest the rest was a little too noisy and informal for me.

There were a lot of "Amens" and "Praise the Lords" through the sermon, and afterward they went into that business of talking in tongues. I felt out of place. Somehow it wasn't my style, though they were truly loving, caring people. But the point of my story is that as I was leaving I noted on the back table a stack of Bibles. A sign read, "IF YOU DON'T OWN A BIBLE, FRIEND, TAKE ONE." Since I didn't own a Bible, I helped myself and stuck a ten-dollar bill on the table. I took it home and began to read it. Never had opened a Bible in my life before. Some of the time I hardly know what it's talking about, but the Old Testament seems to be full of hair-raising and earthy stories, and the New Testament an endless love song to this man Christ. At first it turned me off—His endless wandering about, enticing hardworking tax collectors and fishermen into His utopian cause, but as I read, some of the things He said began to get to me. I found, during the time I have been reading, that some of the knots in my stomach have begun to untangle and I've experienced a strange peace. *(Sybil leans forward with intensity.)* Do you think it's all in my head, Meg?

Sunlight: I'm sure I don't know. I went to Sunday School when I was a little girl. My dad used to drop me off. My mother didn't come from a religious family, but Dad had been carefully raised, and though he'd left it all behind, he had this thing about my going to church. I rather liked it, but when I got into my early teens there were too many other things competing for my attention, so I stopped going. I remember those Old Testament stories quite clearly, and even though they were pretty well edited, I must admit they certainly had punch. I wonder what relation they have to our day, if any, or even if there is a God. Do you think there's a God?

Sybil: Yes, I guess I do, though I have no idea why. Sometimes at night when I sit in my living room looking out at the stars, I have the feeling He knows all about me, and all about the people going by in the cars on the street below.

That's just a hunch, mind you. Bill tells me that civilized people believe in evolution, and that I'm living in the Dark Ages. But all those planets and suns out there. I can't believe it all goes on without any supervision. Even our little planet is so busy with life, how could it all just happen?

But, Meg, I've wandered on and on, and you have to work in the morning. Forgive me for talking so much. I'd best be going now. The next time I'll send you the young woman who cleans for me to sit with the girls, and you must come to my place.

Sunlight: Don't apologize for a thing. I've never discussed my divorce with anyone except my friend Michael, and it did me good to talk about it. Let's get together once a week and just chat. Maybe it'll do us both good.

Sybil: Do you have a Bible?

Sunlight: My dad sent Jenny one for a birthday or Christmas present a few years back. Must be packed away somewhere.

Sybil: Why don't you bring it along? Religion seems to be the thing these days. Maybe we can puzzle it out together—that is if you're interested.

Sunlight: To be perfectly honest, I guess I'm not terribly. But I'm willing to go a few rounds with you as an experiment. Sometimes I feel guilty that I don't send the girls to church, but Sunday is my day to sleep in. We eat a late breakfast and just lounge around.

Sybil: If you can believe that Book, we won't be alone in our study. The Nazarene said where two or three were gathered in His name, He would be with them [Matthew 18:20].

Sunlight: So you think He's going to join us when we try to decipher the Bible? *(She laughs cynically.)*

Sybil: Not literally in the body. But I guess I'd like to believe that His unseen presence might be with us and that it matters to Him whether or not we try to understand whatever it was He was peddling here on earth.

Sunlight *(chuckling):* You better watch it, Sybil, or you'll be as hooked as the fishermen. Shall we make it a week from tonight? Tuesday is good because there's nothing I particularly like on TV and Michael bowls so he never drops by then.

Sybil: Who's this Michael?

Sunlight: Just someone I've known forever. We lived on the same street as children, went to the same schools, and have always been friends. And that's all we are now. He thinks the world is too corrupt for marriage and children, so goes it alone. He's a totally *now* guy, yet inside I suspect he has very old-fashioned principles and is looking for some pure land in which to practice them. My life would be empty without him, and I suppose I'm selfishly pleased that some young lovely hasn't overpowered his convictions and lured him away.

Sybil: I'll look for you next Tuesday then. In the meantime, why don't you browse through the Book of Matthew, and we'll discuss what we've read.

Sunlight: If any of my friends drop by and find me reading the Bible, they'll carry me off to the funny farm. But since the divorce, I'm not exactly swamped with callers. A single woman hasn't much place in today's society. See you Tuesday.

(Sybil, humming, walks down the carpeted hall, and Sunlight checks the children before going to her own room. She rummages through Jennifer's dresser until she finds a small white Bible. After her bedtime preparations she crawls into bed and opens to the Book of Matthew.)

I rejoice this night. Finding no Christian in the city willing to search out Sunlight, Earth Friend has used someone outside the church. How I respect His patience and His compassion. And His ingenuity! With what loving determination He pursues men's hearts. I close my reflections on this day with great joy. And with anticipation. How will Sunlight respond to the teachings of the Prince?

Chapter Three

It is Saturday night again, and Michael asks Sunlight what she'd like to do. She says she is tired and doesn't feel up to dancing—maybe candlelight and some good food—and a drink. A good stiff drink.

Michael: Why a drink?

Sunlight: I don't know. Guess I'm in a black mood. I told you to find a cheerful, uncomplicated date for tonight. I don't think I'll ever be cheerful and uncomplicated again.

Michael: You watch too many late movies, Meg. They're enough to make anyone depressed. You ought to have a hobby or something.

(They are heading through the heavy traffic of downtown Rochester, their destination a restaurant on the west side of town.)

Sunlight: I haven't been watching *any* late movies. I—I've been doing something quite different.

Michael: Like what?

Sunlight: You wouldn't believe me if I told you.

Michael: Try me.

Sunlight: Reading the Bible.

Michael: Like Matthew, Mark, Luke, and John?

Sunlight: No, only Matthew.

Michael: Is that why you are in a black mood?

Sunlight: Indirectly, perhaps. If one were to believe all that stuff, life would never be the same again.

Michael: You mean if you tried to live by it?

Sunlight: Either way. Suppose you believed and ignored

it all? Very scary way to live. Did you ever read Matthew 5? That chapter alone would turn the world upside down if put into practice. What's happening behind all those church doors? Not much, I wager, or surely it would spill out and onto us sinners sooner or later.

Michael: I expect the Christian community *has* made its impact to one degree or another over the years. Don't be too hard on them.

Sunlight: Perhaps—when they died at the stake or were tossed to the lions—but how about now?

Michael: I saw a mass baptism on television the other day. Would that satisfy you?

Sunlight: Oh, Michael, honestly! You see, I met this lady in the building. She's lonely because her husband's a businessman who travels a lot, and she suggested we get together on Tuesday nights and discuss the Bible. It's crazy, because she's not the religious type at all—very chic and sophisticated, but I think she's using the Bible for a tranquilizer. Says she feels better when she reads it. I didn't want to appear too stupid next Tuesday, so I've been really digging into Matthew. It doesn't make *me* feel better. It upsets me somehow. Some of the things Christ said are enough to blow your mind. For instance, He said it's just as bad to hate your brother as to kill him.

Michael: Given his preference, I expect the brother would prefer to be hated.

Sunlight: I guess what Christ was really saying was that it's not enough just to refrain from violence but that we must *love* people as well. He's full of impossible little idealisms like that. But let's forget the whole business. Tonight I want to eat, drink, and be merry. I'm very much of this world, I fear.

I tremble at her words but marvel at her insight. Earth

Friend is pounding home truth as she reads, but in the end, of course, the choice will be hers. Choice—that precious, dangerous freedom.

(The Hitching Post is a lovely place with flowers and fountains and candlelight. Michael and Sunlight, seated in the shadows at a corner table, are a handsome pair. Michael, tall and blond with a spare leanness about him. Dark brown eyes, sober now in his thin, angular face. Sunlight, seated across from him in a soft gold suit, looks vulnerable, unable to relax even in this luxurious setting. Michael sees this and takes her hands.)

Michael: Maggie, just for tonight can't you let go of whatever it is that's eating your insides out? *So you lost Jim.* You're an intelligent, attractive woman with a whole life ahead of you. He isn't the only man on earth. You said you wanted to eat, drink, and be merry. Let's do that. I want to see you smile. Really smile, without all that worry in your eyes.

Sunlight: Then order me a drink.

Michael *(motioning to waiter):*   That's not how your Carpenter Friend handled problems.

Sunlight: Michael, don't bug me about that. I shouldn't have told you. I want steak, rare, and a baked potato. And a tossed salad with the scrumptious dressing they serve here. And a cocktail.

(They eat and they drink and they talk and after a while Sunlight does laugh, her eyes too bright, her voice rising shrilly over the background music. Michael takes her home. At the door she senses his disappointment in the evening.)

Sunlight: You wanted me to laugh, didn't you? There's no laughter in me except what bubbles up out of the alcohol. Go find someone else, Michael. You and the Carpenter would make a good pair. You both have impossible dreams. He tried to *invent* a fantasy world. You're *looking* for one. When you find the pure land, let me know. In the meantime, don't ask me to laugh.

Poor Sunlight! How hurt she is deep at the center of her being, and how tenderly the Prince could heal that hurt. My interest grows in the young man Michael. He exercises great patience toward his perverse little friend. She's quite right that he would make a fine follower of the Prince.

Tuesday night—I have waited for this night with real interest. Every time Sunlight has picked up the phone I've trembled lest she break her appointment with Sybil, but now she hustles the girls into bed. Her Bible lies on the table beside the door, so all is well.

(Carol reads a comic book and Jennifer struggles with a page of remedial math that her teacher has assigned in the hope she will regain her former standing in the class.

Sybil's cleaning girl arrives, and after giving her a few instructions, Sunlight goes down the hall to Sybil's apartment. She gasps a little as she enters, realizing Sybil wasn't joking when she said she sat around thinking up new ways to spend money. The apartment contains a tasteful collection of expensive furniture, art objects, and thick rugs, obviously arranged under the skilled hand of a decorator. A fitting background for Sybil, Sunlight thinks. All the neutral tones accented with black and a whisper of red here and there. Fresh flowers on the glass coffee table. And Sybil in a soft black and white lounging outfit, a red scarf at her throat.)

Sunlight: How do you ever discipline your mind to study in a place like this?

Sybil: I don't see it anymore. Getting this apartment just the way I wanted it occupied me for a long time, but once it was done, I lost interest, though I do love nice things. I'm restless when my surroundings are out of kilter.

Sunlight: You'd better take a tranquilizer when you come to my place, then.

Sybil: I thought your place was cheerful and cleverly done. Undoubtedly, decorating a home presents more of a challenge on a budget, but you've handled it well. Now sink yourself into one of these cream puffs—that's what Bill calls those round velvet chairs—and tell me what you thought of the Book of Matthew.

Sunlight *(for a moment she fumbles for words, then she smiles):* Well, for starters, I thought the man Jesus was extremely impressed with faith. It seemed the only people He could help were those who had a kind of blind trust in Him.

Sybil: Would you believe I was so impressed with the same thing that I began to draw a circle around the word *faith* every time I came to it?

Sunlight: Why do you suppose He expected those people to trust Him? He was a total stranger. He must have had unbelievable magnetism to entice those common working men away from their jobs. Perhaps it wasn't hard to trust in someone like that.

Sybil: Especially after you'd watched Him work a few miracles. What do you think would happen if He came today like that, asking us to believe in Him?

Sunlight: You and Michael would leave everything and march off into the sunset with Him, and I'd be a skeptic and probably lose the good life or whatever it is He's coming to bring us.

Sybil: Speaking of the good life, what did you make of

chapter 24? Half the time I thought He was talking about some catastrophe that was to come upon the city of Jerusalem and then it would seem as if He was talking about the end of our planet altogether.

Sunlight: Maybe it's a mixture of the two. It had to be at least partly about Christ's return to this earth, because it spoke several times about the Son of man coming and described pretty graphically how it would be.

Sybil: It sounded like science fiction. What do you make of it? Do you really think He will ever come again?

Sunlight *(laughing):* Well, the end of that chapter was a sharp warning to the doubter, so you'd *better* believe. Look. It states that the evil servant who says, *even in his heart,* "My lord delayeth his coming," will be cut asunder and have his portion with the hypocrites. Remember, Sybil, Jesus didn't have much time for doubters.

Sybil: If I really dared believe Jesus would return in my day, or even after my death sometime, nothing could depress me. There would be a point to my life, something to get ready for, to look forward to. I guess even death couldn't scare me too much.

Sunlight: You know, I think I *do* believe. That is, I believe that Christ lived, that He was the Son of God, and that He will come back one day to take us—or at least the good people—home.

Sybil: Ah, yes, who are these good people?

Sunlight: I don't know. I was just raised to believe that you had to be good if you wanted to make any points with God. So they must be out there somewhere. In the churches, I suppose.

Sybil: If you believe that, how come you aren't a church member?

Sunlight: It's all too much work. Just reading about it this week sort of got to me. Life is complicated enough without struggling toward some impossible goal.

Sybil: Jesus didn't make it sound like work. I underlined this passage in my Bible: "Come unto me, all ye that labour and are heavy laden, and I will give you *rest*. Take my yoke upon you, and learn of me; for I am meek and lowly in heart: and ye shall find *rest* unto your souls. For my yoke is easy, and my burden is light" [Matthew 11:28-30*].

Sunlight: But a yoke is still a yoke, and a burden a burden. And who wants any more burdens? He also said, "He that taketh not his cross, and followeth after me is not worthy of me" [Matthew 10:38]. A cross is not comfortable, Sybil.

Sybil: Yet those men He called followed Him gladly and mourned when He died. It brought them no wealth, so they must have found something in His company that made the poverty and inconvenience all worthwhile. He gave them something better than security. What do you suppose it was?

(Sybil brings out a pot of tea, and they chat about other things for a few moments but soon have their Bibles open again.)

Sunlight: Did you notice in Matthew 19:16-22 that one young man He invited to follow Him didn't go?

Sybil: Because he was rich. That kind of scared me. Made me wonder how much all this means to me—my home, my charge cards, my Lincoln.

Sunlight: He didn't dare to believe that what Christ offered could possibly be as fulfilling as his role of Mr. Big in the community. You've already told me, Sybil, that money hasn't made you happy, so why would you even hesitate?

Sybil: I'll bet you wouldn't leave the security of your job or your own cozy little apartment.

---

*Emphasis in the Bible texts has been supplied by the author.

Sunlight *(smiling):*   I'd have asked Him right out what was in it for me. And I already know His answer—for I noted He never promised anyone immediate rewards. Somewhere here in chapter 10 [verse 22] He said they would be hated by all men for His sake, but if they endured to the end, they would be saved. And another time He promised the disciples they would sit upon thrones and have a part in the judgment and that anyone who gave up a lot for Him would receive a generous reward and have everlasting life [Matthew 19:28, 29]. But all that was for the future. He promised them only headaches on this earth, and I have enough of them already.

Sybil: My favorite passage in the whole Book of Matthew was chapter 9, verse 36: "When he saw the multitudes, he was moved with compassion on them." I'll bet the fishermen felt that, and it was so warm and comforting that the almighty dollar lost its appeal.

Did you notice that when Christ died on the cross, an earthquake opened the graves of some of the saints and they came to life and went into the city [Matthew 27:52, 53]? I thought good people went to heaven when they died. But if that's the case, why did they come out of the ground? Meg, I'm boiling with questions.

Sunlight: I noticed that too. I also wondered what it meant when it said, "In the end of the Sabbath, as it began to dawn toward the first day of the week" [Matthew 28:1]. I thought the Sabbath *was* the first day of the week. At least I remember my grandfather calling Sunday the Sabbath. My head was spinning when I finished studying, Sybil. Saturday night when Michael and I went out, I wasn't very good company. Maybe we shouldn't study anymore. Let's just get together and chat or go out and take some macrame lessons or something. This stuff is way over our heads.

Sybil *(obviously disappointed):* I don't think it's meant to be. We've studied only one week, and I thought we discovered some exciting things. More than I imagined we would. Couldn't we try a few more sessions? Why don't you ask Michael about this Sabbath thing? What's his business, anyway?

Sunlight: He has his degree in behavioral science and works in the social services department for the city. I doubt he knows a thing about religion. His big concern is equality for minority groups. That's a kind of religion, I suppose. Do *you* believe, Sybil?

Sybil: I'm not ready to give a definite answer to that yet. When I'm reading about Christ living here on this planet, I'm pretty convinced, but Bill shakes me a bit when he calls it all a charming myth. You know, Meg, it isn't enough to simply believe anyhow.

Sunlight: Huh? Why do you say that?

Sybil: Because when I was just skipping around in the Bible, before I met you, I ran across a funny verse in James. It said that even the devils believe and tremble [James 2:19].

Sunlight: So where does that put us?

Sybil: I puzzled over that a long time one night. Finally, all of a sudden, it occurred to me that most of those people who came to Jesus to be healed had to leave their homes and make the effort to find Him. Some had to have others carry them on stretchers. It wasn't easy to get through the crowds that surrounded Him. If they had just stayed at home *and believed,* even though He was right in their town, they would never have been healed. *So maybe we have to come to Him.*

Sunlight: Well, how do we do that?

Sybil: Like we're doing here tonight, I think, searching the Bible to find out what He was like and how He wants us to live. I don't know a thing about prayer, but Jesus felt it necessary to keep in touch with His Father when He was on earth, so maybe there really is something to getting on your knees and trying to make contact. It boggles my mind to think that God could find Sybil Norris on His radar and listen to what she has to say.

Sunlight: But we aren't sick. Are you sure we need to find Him?

Sybil: You know, I think this whole planet is sick. Sick with loneliness and fear and despair. Can you find yourself in that picture?

Sunlight *(sadly):* Middle section, front row.

Sybil: Me too. So maybe He has something to offer us, if we're willing to expose ourselves to Him. Do you know how to pray?

Sunlight: Now I lay me down to sleep . . . .

Sybil: I'm serious, Meg. *Really* pray.

Sunlight: I've always had a feeling it's only a matter of stating your case. I don't think there are any rules, unless you're holding high mass at St. James Cathedral.

Sybil: Then how about demonstrating? I really think we're crazy to try to understand the Bible without help, so ask Him to give us some direction this next week as we study. OK?

Sunlight: Right now?

Sybil: Why not? I'd do it myself, only I'm—I'm too shy.

Sunlight *(head bowed):* Lord, we are blundering around in the Bible and coming up with a lot of questions and not many answers. But we do have a shaky sort of faith in You. If that faith is acceptable to You, please help it to grow and help us in our study. Amen.

Sybil: Thanks. Maybe next week *I'll* try. Now hurry home and hop into bed. You need your rest. Let's try to wade through the Book of Mark this next week.

I am too moved to write. I have heard Sunlight's first prayer, and knowing the Prince as I do, I can assure you He rejoices, and Earth Friend will put all His powers at their disposal. Oh, that every being on earth would open his Bible as those two have tonight. Earth Friend's power would flash across that small planet, and the Prince would soon have a people made ready for the homecoming. I go now to find Him. I must share my joy with someone, and none will understand better than He. Then I shall speak to Sunlight's Recording Angel, for his heart, too, must have been made glad this night.

Chapter Four

It is one of those bleak November nights on Planet Earth, bleak at least in the city of Rochester, New York, where across the black expanse of Lake Ontario, winds bring a fine biting snow, tossing it over the city in blinding gusts of white. Sunlight, clearing her tiny, immaculate kitchen, hears its thin tattoo against the window and shivers inwardly. Snow can be cozy when it shuts two in together but just the opposite when one is alone. She is not really alone, of course. Her girls, excited by snow as all earth children seem to be, have their noses pressed against the large living-room window, watching the flakes fall on the sidewalk below. It is indeed a lovely sight. I, too, am a bit fascinated by falling snow and wish I might stand with them, my arms about them, for I love Sunlight's daughters. I would like them to know that though they may be missing one parent, all heaven is concerned about them. That they need have no fears, no insecurity.

The phone rings. Carol leaps to answer it, smiles at the voice on the other end, and announces happily to her mother that Michael is bringing over some corn to pop. When he arrives a half hour later, snow clings to his jacket and his hair. The girls brush him off and frisk him for the popcorn, which they soon have in the popper. When they sit together later, watching television, Carol curls up in Michael's lap and Jenny snuggles by her mother.

Sunlight: If you aren't careful, Michael, that one will domesticate you yet.

Michael: I'm all for domestication, Maggie, but only when the conditions are right.

Carol: I wish you didn't talk in big words I can't understand. What does *domesticate* mean?

Michael: It means using your charms to entice a poor, helpless young man to sit beside the fire munching popcorn forever.

Carol: Sounds OK to me.

Michael *(laughing):* You women are all the same.

Sunlight: You really should settle down beside someone's fire pretty soon, Michael. You aren't getting any younger, and look how great you are with children.

Michael: Is that an invitation?

Sunlight: No, Silly. I'm endangering a perfectly good friendship by urging you into marriage—to someone else.

Michael: I've told you, Meg, it's a nasty world. If these two little gals were mine, I wouldn't sleep nights for what's ahead of them. If it's OK with you, I'll just help you worry when the time comes.

Sunlight: Don't say I didn't warn you, when you're a lonely old man in a nursing home without kith or kin. Now you girls hit the bed. You've stalled long enough.

(The girls go off to their bedroom, and Sunlight gathers up dishes and picks stray pieces of popcorn off the floor.)

Michael: Does that mean it's time for me to go too?

Sunlight: No, Michael, sit and chat a bit. These snowy nights make me edgy.

Michael: Remember when your dad used to drive a carload of us out to Chad's Hill on Saturday nights when we were kids? You loved the snow then. You were little and intense like Carol, and you'd stand with your face turned up to the sky, just letting the flakes fall on your cheeks. The rest of us would laugh at you, but you didn't mind. You were enchanted with the magic of winter and didn't care a whit for our laughter. It's still the same now, Maggie.

Sunlight: But I'm not the same girl, Michael. A little of the enchantment has rubbed off life as well as wintertime. Tell me about your work, all the trials of the suffering city. Maybe it will make me feel good by comparison.

Michael: I don't really want to talk about it. Sometimes I think I'm in the wrong business. The stories that pass over my desk are depressing. They make me wonder what it's all about anyway. By the way, how's your friendship with Sybil coming?

Sunlight: She's quite a lady. I'm glad she was persistent. I realize now I had shut myself away from everyone but you, and probably would have shut you out, too, if you'd have let me. It feels good to have a friend again, and I like the gal. She has a good mind and doesn't play any games. I guess about all we've learned about the Bible is how ignorant we are. You need some kind of base to build on. Everything we read just creates more questions in our minds.

By the way, how come, when some women visited Christ's tomb, it says they went after the Sabbath as the first day of the week was beginning to dawn? I thought the Sabbath *was* the first day of the week.

Michael: There's a simple answer, Meg, and you know it yourself if you stop and think. What day do the Jews keep?

Sunlight: Saturday.

Michael: And what nationality was Jesus?

Sunlight: A Jew—of course. How stupid of me. So *He* kept Saturday, and so did all those other people we were reading about. I just never thought about that.

Michael: Christians observe Sunday today in honor of Christ's resurrection, which took place on the first day of the week, as you read. Probably He Himself gave instruction for the change, if you look for it.

Sunlight: Well, that will give me something to tell Sybil.

You know what I'd like, Michael? I'd like you to read me the last three chapters in the Book of Mark. That book is our assignment for this week, and I've not quite finished. I'll just close my eyes and try to visualize it as you read. I think it's about the trial and crucifixion of Christ.

(Sunlight hands Michael the small white Bible, and he reads, his voice quiet and steady against the rising wind outside. When he finishes, Sunlight speaks.)

Sunlight: You should have studied for the priesthood, seeing you're going the monastic route anyhow. You read it so well, I was right there watching everything that happened to Christ. You know, I've come to the conclusion that the cross was either the focal point of all time or the greatest hoax anyone has ever pulled off.

Michael: As I read, I thought it was strange I'd never read those words before—never read a word in the entire Bible for that matter. I picked up a little of the historical background of those times in college but somehow have never held the Book in my hand until this moment. Somehow, I felt deeply moved. I don't think it was a hoax, Maggie.

Sunlight: If you really believed on Him, you would have to make changes in your life. Everyone He called had to be willing to change, to learn His new life-style, to walk away from old things. I'm almost afraid to believe for what He might ask of me.

Michael: I think I'd like Him to ask something of me. A difficult thing that would startle me out of my rut. But those are easy words, and how did we get off onto this anyhow? What would you like to do Saturday night?

Sunlight: *You* choose. You always leave it up to me, and I either dance myself into exhaustion or drink too much.

Michael: How about something simple then, like going skating at the outdoor rink downtown?

Sunlight: Hey, that's neat. I'd love it. I haven't had a pair of skates on in years, but I bet I'm still good.

Michael: How about taking the girls along? We knew how to skate long before we were their age.

Sunlight: Michael, what a friend you are! They will proba- bly fold up with excitement before the night ever arrives. *(Michael leaves, and Sunlight makes ready for bed.)*

It is strange indeed to think there are decent young men like Michael, who have never held a Bible in their hands. That Book is man's opportunity to peek into heaven, to know why he is on Planet Earth and how to survive his predicament. It would seem men and women would be poring over the Bible every spare moment, but they live as though their meager seventy-five-year life spans (if they're lucky) are all that matter. They mourn if their favorite television show is canceled for an evening, yet ignore the vital things concerning eternity. The Prince explained to me that the Rebel beclouds the minds of earthlings until they can hardly comprehend their danger. Only Earth Friend can penetrate that cloud, and most reject His attempts. Sybil was one of the rare ones who was ripe to be delivered from Rebel's power. Thank God she shared with Sunlight. That took courage.

(It is Tuesday evening and Sybil and Sunlight sit at the small kitchen table in Sunlight's apartment. Sunlight has a red pencil poised above her Bible.)

Sunlight: I find I can't read without this pencil. I'm con- stantly finding things I want to underline. There are some astonishing things in this Book. Sometimes I get stuck on one verse, and it's so mind-blowing I never get any further at that sitting. Guess I'd never have finished if Michael hadn't read me the last three chapters the other night.

Sybil: Does he think we have lost our minds?

Sunlight: On the contrary, I think he was quite impressed with what Mark had to say, and also with the man Jesus. Michael would have been an ardent follower of Christ, because he believes so strongly in causes.

Sybil: Would he like to study with us?

Sunlight: He's a very private person. I think he'd be aghast at our brainstorming, but he'll listen to anything I want to share with him and give it careful thought.

Sybil: I'm sure you realize, Child, that the man is in love with you.

Sunlight *(silent for a moment):* It's not like you think, Sybil. We share a lot of memories—right back to sandbox days, in fact. He's lonely—I'm lonely. For now, we meet each other's needs. That's all there is to it. Sooner or later he will meet someone who will sweep him off his feet, and he'll ditch all his altruistic notions.

(Sybil only smiles.)

Sunlight: I never knew before that Matthew, Mark, Luke, and John were simply four men telling their own versions of the same story. I am probably the last person on earth to find that out. It would seem to make for very boring reading, but I found myself going back and forth between Matthew and Mark, comparing their accounts, and it turned out to be fascinating. To what great thoughts did Mark inspire you?

Sybil: That Christ couldn't move without stumbling over someone. He had no privacy. It said here in chapter 6, verse 31, that Christ suggested He and His disciples go to an isolated place to rest awhile, "for there were many coming and going, and they had no leisure so much to eat." But even then, when they arrived at their destination "the people saw them departing, and many knew him, and ran afoot thither out of all cities, and outwent them, and came together unto him. And Jesus, when he came out, saw much people, and was moved with compassion toward them, because they were as sheep not having a shepherd: and he began to teach them many things" [verses 33, 34].

And here, further on in the same chapter [verses 53, 56], it says, "And when they had passed over, they came into the land of Gennesaret, and drew to the shore. And when they were come out of the ship, straightway they knew him, and ran through that whole region round about, and began to carry about in beds those that were sick, where they heard he was. And whithersoever he entered, into villages, or cities, or country, they laid the sick in the streets, and besought him that they might touch if it were but the border of his garment: and as many as touched him were made whole."

Meg, when I read those verses I wept. I saw humanity clawing at Jesus, fascinated by His teachings, greedy for His loaves and fishes, scrabbling for His healing touch— imagining even the border of His robe was magic. I felt His hunger, His weariness. He must have been turned off sometimes by their grabbing—*yet there is the record:* He "*was moved with compassion* toward them, because they were as sheep not having a shepherd." He simply couldn't walk away and abandon them.

If He feels the same way about our generation today, He must be sick with frustration, for instead of clutching at Him today, we are arrogant and indifferent. I have a feeling that is worse.

But anyhow, to get back to the multitudes, I found a verse in chapter 14 that broke my heart: "And immediately, while he yet spake, cometh Judas, one of the twelve, and with him *a great multitude* with swords and staves, from the chief priests and the scribes and the elders" [verse 43].

For three years Christ had touched those pushing, shoving mobs with His healing hands—and He did touch them, too, no matter how diseased or filthy—had taught them when He was exhausted and faint with hunger, and now a *multitude* comes out to take Him with swords and staves. It just wasn't fair, Meg.

And before that, when He was in the Garden praying and agonizing over what lay ahead, they slept. His best friends slept! [Mark 14:33-42]. Can you imagine? (*Sybil's cheeks are flushed and her eyes shiny with tears.*)

Sunlight: I was deeply moved as I read this week too. In fact, the Book of Mark worked a minor miracle in my life.

Sybil: Then tell me about it—quickly.

Sunlight: Go back to—here—chapter 11, verses 24-26. Listen. "Therefore I say unto you, What things soever ye desire, when ye pray, believe that ye receive them, and ye shall have them. And when ye stand praying, *forgive,* if ye have ought against any: that your Father also which is in heaven may forgive you your trespasses. But if ye do not forgive, neither will your Father which is in heaven forgive your trespasses."

Well, this past week I have been praying each morning. Just a simple prayer for the girls, then that you and I would understand what we are studying, and for forgiveness of my sins. I don't care much for the bitter, sharp-tongued person I've become over the past two years.

So when I read those verses about God not hearing us if we cannot forgive our fellowmen, it was like a slap in the face. As plainly as if God had written me a letter, I saw the awful ugliness I feel for Jim, plus the jealousy and hatred I have for his wife. Suddenly the anger and hurt and bitterness that were bottled up inside me poured out. I cried for hours. Luckily the girls were in bed. I lay down on the living-room rug and sobbed. And dug my fingers so hard into the shag that the next morning half my nails were broken. In my mind I screamed at Jim all the things I had wanted to say so long—horrible, ugly things. And then I cried harder than ever, for I realized that under the anger was the most awful hurt. I had never looked at it before. I guess I hadn't dared. It hit me then that to have hurt so badly, I must have loved a lot. And how could I feel so bitter toward someone I loved so much. I knew there in the darkness that I would always care deeply for him and be concerned for his happiness, but I prayed a new prayer, Sybil—that God would help me to forgive Jim and erase all the bitterness from my heart.

When I got myself together I went straight to the phone and called Jim's home. Marie—that's his wife—answered, and I asked her if she and Jim would like to have dinner with the girls and me Sunday. It took her by surprise, and I know she was uncomfortable, but she checked with Jim and said they'd love to come.

Now I rather doubt they were all that enthusiastic, but I want to make things more normal for Jim and the girls, and we have to start somewhere. I've asked Michael to come and would like you and Bill to join us, if he's home. If he's not, just come by yourself. I think it will be less awkward for everyone if it's a little dinner party. I used to be great at dinner parties but haven't entertained anyone in months—so that's what the Book of Mark did for me.

Sybil: Surely you touched the healing hem of His garment, Meg. I'm sitting here covered with goose bumps at your story.

Sunlight: Well, I'd hardly call myself healed. I feel pretty uneasy about Sunday. My reactions are far from what they should be toward Jim and Marie, but the girls are ecstatic, and a great weight has rolled from my shoulders, now that I can admit what I feel is more hurt than anger. Can you come?

Sybil: Bill will be home that day, and I think he will humor me because he's been gone so much lately. I want you to meet him. I've made him sound dreadful, but he's a very special man when he wants to be.

Sunlight: Do you love him?

Sybil: Unfortunately, yes.

Sunlight: Why unfortunately?

Sybil: Because I would have long ago built myself a more rewarding life if my heart didn't start leaping around in my chest on those rare occasions when he comes walking through my door.

(She pauses, as if reluctant to dwell upon a painful subject.)

Sunlight: You really did your homework this week. You put me to shame.

Sybil *(chuckling):* Remember, I have a lot more time than you do, and this whole thing has given purpose to my days. *(She glances at her watch.)*

It's ten o'clock, and we've hardly scratched the surface. What did you learn?

Sunlight: You know, I can hardly believe it, but I don't dread those hours after the girls are in bed anymore. I find myself looking forward to the quiet time when I open the Bible. And I especially look forward to these nights when we share what we've studied. I'm so glad you spoke to me in the elevator that day.

Sybil: But you didn't answer my question. What did we learn?

Sunlight: I learned from Him that I can afford to love Jim even if he no longer loves me back. Christ did that, you know, in loving us. He even loved those who crucified Him.

I have to admit that I don't have good feelings all the time. One night I was watching television and didn't feel like reading the Bible at all. *M.A.S.H.* and the Book of Mark seemed light-years apart. Totally unrelated. It's very easy to get disconnected from religion, I fear.

Sybil: I don't like the word *religion*. It sounds like bingo games and church suppers. I like what you and I have right here. I fear if we tried to fit it into a mold, a denominational mold, that it might slip right through our fingers.

Tonight *I'm* going to pray. You won't laugh if I'm not eloquent?

Sunlight: Promise.

Sybil: We come to You with delight, Lord, and with awe and love. Will You teach us how to serve You? Will You give us the kind of faith that pleased You so much when You found it on earth? Please be in Meg's home and in mine. Amen.

Sunlight: That was a beautiful prayer, Sybil. Let's not spoil it by chatting. Just let yourself out, and I'll see you Sunday about 1:00.

I should be thrilled—and I am—but I tremble for those two newborn babes. The Rebel is furious at what is happening and will never allow them to continue to learn and grow unmolested. His brilliant and evil mind is already scheming to destroy Earth Friend's work. If they will only continue to pray and study, no matter how the Rebel batters them, all his plottings will be in vain—but it is not easy for earthlings, for they cannot see the drama going on behind the scenes. They can only trust in the Prince, and that's often difficult when their world begins to crumble. I long to leave a little note on Sunlight's pillow tonight, saying, "Hold on, Friend. Just hold on. No matter what comes." But that is not my privilege. All that can be done for her, the Prince and Earth Friend will have to do.

Chapter Five

(In the dining area of Sunlight's living room the table is set for eight. Sunlight arranges flowers while Carol brushes Jenny's long hair.)

Carol: I'm so excited, Mom. We're having our first real live party in our own apartment, and Daddy's coming.

Jenny: It's not going to be quite like old times, Dummy. His wife will be here, too, and you mustn't talk about things that happened when we all lived together.

Carol: Mom, make her stop treating me like a two-year-old.

Sunlight: I guess we both have to realize Carol isn't a baby anymore, Jen. I think she understands the situation. I'm not quite sure myself what we *are* going to talk about. *(She pauses.)* Would you girls think I was insane if we prayed that this will be a happy, relaxed time for everyone? Right here, now, before the guests arrive?

Jenny: What's going on with you and Sybil? Are you getting religious like the old lady that helped you clean when we lived in Pennfield?

Sunlight: I'm not sure what it means to "get religious," Jen, but Sybil and I *have been* trying to find out what it means to follow God. In fact, knowing God just a little bit gave me the courage to have this dinner party today, and to ask your father, so something good has come from it.

Carol: Then let's pray. We could stand a lot more good things around here.

(Sunlight kneels, and the girls kneel uncertainly beside her.)

Sunlight: God, I feel a little scared at what I have set out to do. I'm not sure just how to put everyone at ease when the guests arrive. Please send Your peace into this room, and may each guest feel Your love—and please give me the gift of a forgiving heart. Amen.

Carol: That's the first time I ever prayed in my life.

Sunlight: Which doesn't say much for my mothering.

(The doorbell rings. Sunlight welcomes Sybil and Bill.)

Sybil: Meg, I want you to meet my husband, Bill.

Bill *(a tall, distinguished-appearing man with piercing, intelligent eyes):*   I am in your debt, young lady, for keeping Sybil entertained these past weeks. I never expected to see her so fascinated with the Bible. She's been reading it lately like it contained her horoscope for the day.

Sunlight *(laughing):*   We're complete novices, floundering in very deep water, I fear. Sit down and help yourselves to some of those dips on the coffee table.

(The doorbell rings again. Enter Jim and Marie.)

Sunlight *(hesitantly to Jim):*   I thought it was about time I started entertaining again before I forgot all my best recipes. Thank you for coming.

Jim *(smiling but uncomfortable):*   I'm still in a state of shock, but thank you for inviting us. Meg, this is Marie.

Sunlight *(extending her hand):*   I'm sorry it's taken me so long to get myself together. Please relax and enjoy yourself. Jen, would you take Marie's coat, please?

(Sunlight goes into the kitchen and leans against the wall, taking a deep breath and talking to herself.)

Sunlight: I made it. For two years I've lived in terror of even looking at her, and I survived. O God, help me not to hate her.

(Michael steps through the kitchen door.)

Sunlight: You startled me. I'm recuperating from the first round and readying for the next. Oh, Michael, it hurts so bad. *(Tears run down her face.)*

Michael: I'm glad to hear you say those words, Maggie. It's step No. 1. Now what can I do to help you? Besides finding a Kleenex.

(Together they ready the table, with Jenny and Carol helping. The dinner proceeds, awkwardly at first, but with increasing warmth and laughter. Sunlight busies herself with serving and says little.)

Jim: The world of science is changing so fast that the textbooks my classes use are outdated almost before they leave their wrappers.

Sybil: Maybe they should dispense with them altogether and just have daily bulletins from the laboratories *(laughter)*.

Michael *(smiling):* Doesn't it seem strange to you that all of a sudden men would get it all together, after thousands of years of crude existence? Maybe we humans aren't as brilliant as we'd like to think. Suppose there's a Power beyond us shaping events to fit His master plan?

Bill: You are suggesting, I gather, that history might be coming to some kind of a conclusion. I'm not sure I want things to wind up. I'm just getting to the place where I can enjoy the rewards of a lifetime of work.

Sybil: Don't you think whatever lies ahead might be just as pleasant and challenging as whatever it is you plan to do?

Bill: I wouldn't bank on it. It's always been my opinion that we'd best get all that's to be had out of this life, because I figure we're little but fertilizer when it's over.

Marie: I couldn't enjoy life here if I believed that. There is so much beauty, and human relationships are so precious. Life must go on somehow.

(Sunlight watches Marie's delicately pretty face, now intense and serious.)

Jim: I feel the same way sometimes in the lab. Life is so mysterious and complex that it would be insane to destroy it. But I haven't the faintest idea where we're all heading. I just do the best I can and hope everything turns out all right.

Sybil: I think that's a dangerous approach, Jim. Meg and I have been studying the Bible, and I'm convinced that more's expected of us than just living a decent life. In fact, Christ said we must love the Lord with all our hearts and our neighbors as ourselves. I doubt we understand what it means to truly love our neighbors, much less to love the Lord with all our hearts. Most of us barely acknowledge His existence.

Bill: This conversation is getting far too heavy for me. C'mon, Jenny. Let's excuse ourselves and read the comics. I haven't seen Flash Gordon for at least ten years.

Jenny *(giggling):* I don't think he's around anymore.

Bill: Well, that's a shame, but surely Blondie hasn't retired.
(They settle down on the couch with the Sunday paper.)

Jim: We have to go, Meg. Marie has some artwork to prepare for the Christmas play at school. You're still the best cook in western New York. *(He turns to Carol.)* Come here, Baby. Give your pa a little lovin' before he has to go.
(Carol climbs delightedly into his lap.)
(Gradually the guests drift away until only Michael remains.)

Sunlight: How did I do?

Michael: Only you can tell. How *did* you do?

Sunlight: Well, I didn't lie down on the floor and kick my heels and cry. Maybe that's pretty good for the first time.

Michael *(tenderly):* It was more than pretty good, Maggie. It was splendid. I have something for you.

Sunlight: Animal, vegetable, or mineral?

Michael: Beats me. *(He places a beautiful, leatherbound*

Bible in her hands.)

Sunlight: Michael! How did you know? I've wanted one so badly, and they are so expensive.

Michael: As I think you could tell at dinner, I've been doing a little studying myself, and I find that you can't get anywhere without a concordance. That thing you were using was only a child's New Testament.

Sunlight: You are so good to me. I have a feeling this may be the best gift anyone's ever given me. But I'm dying of curiosity. Whatever possessed you to start reading the Bible?

Michael: Those few chapters I read to you that night here really got to me. It was as though they met some need I'd had all my life. I went out the next day and bought a Bible and have been digging away ever since.

Sunlight: Do you want to study with Sybil and me?

Michael: No, thanks anyway, but I have to wrestle it out alone. It will either turn my life upside down or I'll go my way without it. (*He pauses.*) Somehow, I can't see how one can become moderately involved.

Sunlight: It almost frightens me to hear you say that, for that's how I feel too. I'm not sure I'm ready to give myself totally to anything, yet it may be already too late for me to turn back.

(*Michael and the girls help Sunlight tidy the house, then he leaves. The girls sit on the couch looking gingerly at Sunlight's new Bible.*)

Jenny: They make it seem so mysterious by putting it in soft leather and with the pages so thin. Are you sure it's any different from any other book?

Sunlight: You can buy it in paperback at most bookstores, Love. But that doesn't make it any less special. If it's really God's message to us, it *deserves* fine pages wrapped in soft leather.

Jenny: Do you think it's really God's message to us?

Sunlight: Well, I've heard some say it's the only intelligent inkling we have of where we came from, why we're here, and where we're headed.

Jenny *(giggling):* Do you know the answers to all those questions?

Sunlight: No, Jen. I wish I did. But Sybil and I are searching. And Michael too. So among us, maybe we'll find out.

Jenny: Could I understand it?

Sunlight: Some parts, I'm sure. Get ready for bed and bring your own Bible, the one we've been using, and we'll read the first chapter of Luke together.

Carol: Me too?

Sunlight: Sure, Button, but it may be over your head.
(They read about half of the long first chapter of Luke, Sunlight taking time to explain or admitting she herself doesn't understand.)

Carol: It must have been great to have been chosen the mother of Jesus, or that other guy, John. Maybe better than being a television star or an Olympic champion.

Jenny: Why do you suppose Mary got picked, Mom?

Sunlight: I guess because God saw in her those qualities that would give His Son the best start in His earth life. It would have scared me a little, I guess.

Jenny: Could we do this every night?

Sunlight: Perhaps now and then when you don't have too much schoolwork. Now scoot.

Carol: If I kneel down by my bed, could I talk to Jesus?

Sunlight: Of course.

Carol: What do I say?

Sunlight: Anything you'd like to say if He were sitting right there beside you.

I have seen a lot of dinner parties on Planet Earth, but

none that interested me so much as the one I just observed. I would not have believed Sunlight capable of playing the gracious hostess to her former husband and his wife. Only Earth Friend's softening influence could bring about such a change. She will not heal easily, but the closer she comes to the Prince, the less earth-pain will matter.

I long to talk to the Prince about it all, but His ministry in the sanctuary [Hebrews 8:1, 2] consumes most of His time. I wish I could take Sunlight, Sybil, and Michael on a tour of this city. If they could have but one glimpse, they would have no doubts. The countless angels surrounding the throne of God [Revelation 5:11], the seraphim singing, "Holy, holy, holy, is the Lord of hosts" [Isaiah 6:2, 3], and the spirit of peace and joy in the heart of every inhabitant. Sometimes when we angels sing His praise, it seems to me there are no words or notes grand enough.

When the Prince first returned to heaven, there was great celebration and rejoicing as He was seated at the right hand of the Father, but the work of salvation was not yet done, and He soon moved into His role as Intercessor for His human family. Now, though His intercession still goes on, He has added to that the work of judgment [Daniel 7:9, 10, 13, 14], for the decision must be made regarding the eternal destiny of each human being before the Prince can bring His people home.

Earthlings could learn so much if they would turn off their TVs and put away their books and magazines. The Bible is brimming over with exciting discoveries.

The Book of Daniel is filled with fascinating prophecy that sheds insight right down through the ages to the end. One would think men would spend every spare moment searching and praying for understanding when it involves their eternal destiny, but the Rebel somehow soothes them into a lethal indifference. We know the day will come when the Prince will walk away from His work as both Intercessor and Judge, and at that time earthlings will no longer have the freedom to choose between the Rebel and the Prince. Their choices will have been made and their decisions sealed for eternity.

Sometimes I look at that small planet, clouds drifting across its deep blue surface, and wonder how much time it has left. How many more sunrises it will see. How many more times the leaves will fall and blow across the winding roads. How many more mornings women will rise and wake their sleeping families to ready for the day. How many more springtimes will green the frozen land. And I weep because I love them.

Chapter Six

(Scene: Sybil's living room, Tuesday evening. Bill is home, and he and Sybil are awaiting Sunlight's arrival.)

Bill: Why don't you stop plumping pillows and fussing around, so I can talk with you? Meg will soon be here.

Sybil: If I'd had any idea you'd still be home, I'd have canceled her visit. Are you sure you don't mind that she's coming?

Bill: Heaven knows, Syb, it's your home, and you've had to entertain yourself in it for years. Who am I to criticize the life-style you've built in my absence? Besides, I rather like Meg and admire her cool. That little dinner she threw on Sunday couldn't have been easy for her.

Sybil: Bill, why have you been home these past few days? What's going on at the office? It isn't like you to sleep late and lounge around with the newspaper. Is something wrong? Are you ill?

Bill *(laughing):* Most wives scold if their men are away from home. You never did that, but you're scolding now because I'm here. That's a switch.

Sybil: I'm not scolding, and you know it, but something is going on. Now out with it.

Bill: We have a few minutes before Meg's due. Come here, Sybil, and sit down beside me. I want to talk with you.

Sybil *(seating herself on couch):* You haven't talked to me about anything but business in the past thirty years, Bill, so whatever you're going to say has to be important. You're frightening me a bit.

Bill: There's nothing to fear. The past few weeks I've been having an occasional stab of pain in my chest, so I went to a specialist and had the works. He didn't find anything of any consequence but said I had to slack off and get out from under the pressure. Insisted I take a month off. So you're stuck with me for a while.

Sybil: You mean you aren't going to the office for a month!

Bill: Think you can survive?

Sybil: Oh, Bill . . . *(Her eyes fill with tears, and she cannot go on.)*

Bill *(taking her hand):* I've been doing a lot of thinking the past few days about the way I've treated you for years, just dashing in and out and assuming you were OK because you didn't complain. I'd almost forgotten what a special woman you are. At that little get-together at Meg's the other day, neither of those young women could hold a candle to you. You're a beauty, Sybil, and I've taken it for granted far too long. I've thought about the early days of our marriage when we didn't have a nickel and how I longed to give you everything. That became my obsession. Then after a while I fear it wasn't for you anymore. I just fell in love with money for its own sake, not for what it could do for us, but only to watch it pile up and know it was all mine.

Even before I went to the doctor, I'd been thinking that it was about time to quit. All those airports and restaurants were beginning to get to me. But it's hard to slow down when you've been running for thirty years. Can you understand that, Syb?

Sybil: Yes.

Bill: I want to get off the roller coaster, but you've got to help me. We could travel together. No more deadlines and conferences. Just you and me relaxing in Europe, moving on when we felt like it, seeing the sights. Coming home when we got good and ready. It won't be for a while because I've got this month of enforced rest and then I'll have to tie up the loose ends of the business and turn it over to someone else.

Sybil: I don't care if we have to live on a budget as tight as our first one on Marcy Street, if you'll just be home. Remember that dingy little apartment?

Bill: Don't worry, Woman. There'll be no budget. The rat race has paid off, and we're set for whatever years we have left.

Sybil: I'm worried about the chest pains.

Bill: The doctor said they were simply a warning, nothing more. You are not to mess up the good years we have ahead by fretting.

Sybil: Bill, I want you to share the exciting things Meg and I are learning from the Bible. I know you make light of religion, but surely you must believe there's a God. I would rather have you study the Bible with me than take me to Paris. You will sit in on our discussion tonight? Please?

Bill: I'd do most anything to make you happy, but you must not ask that of me. The Bible means no more to me than a collection of fairy tales. You and Meg go right ahead, if this brings you pleasure, but count me out. I'll be in the den watching TV.

Sybil: But you'll be bored.

Bill: Well, it's a lot better being bored at home than in a lonely motel somewhere.

(Bill leaves the room and Sybil sits with a troubled look until the doorbell rings. She welcomes Meg and shares with her the news of Bill's retirement.)

Sunlight: Sybil, that's wonderful. It means you won't ever be alone again. Are you sure it's OK that I came tonight?

Sybil: I tried to get him to join us, but he has no interest in religion whatever. He's in the den watching TV and didn't seem to mind that you were coming. I just feel sort of numb. It hasn't quite hit me yet that he'll be around. I guess I'm not really letting myself believe it for fear he'll find it too dull and go back to work, chest pains and all. I just have to keep him happy, Meg, *somehow*.

Sunlight: The way he looks at you, I'd say you were doing fine.

Sybil: Well, let's get down to business. I've been looking forward to this all week, though it's been harder to find time to study with Bill around. He always wants to go to a movie or go out for dinner or have some friends in. I finally found that early morning was the only time I could study, so I've been getting up at 7:00. It's lovely then these winter mornings, and my mind seems clear and ready to learn. Bill doesn't get up until nearly 10:00, so I have plenty of time.

Sunlight: Luke's a long book, and I didn't quite finish, but I read chapter 15 over and over. I think it will always be my favorite portion of the Bible. It was like a personal letter from God to me, as a new believer. Let me read you verse 7: "I say unto you, that likewise *joy shall be in heaven over one sinner that repenteth,* more than over ninety and nine just persons, which need no repentance."

Do you realize, Sybil, that means that heaven is rejoicing over us? Something really happened up there because of two nobodies like us? Jesus told three stories in that chapter, and they were all about the joy God feels when we respond to Him. I loved the story of the shepherd and the lost sheep. I thought about it all week at work. When the shepherd found the sheep he didn't scold and knock it around. He didn't whip it along in front of him in a fit of anger at the inconvenience it had caused or tie a rope around its neck and drag it behind him over the rocky path. Read it, Sybil. It says, "He layeth it on his shoulders, rejoicing" [verse 5]. I don't think we know anything about that kind of love here on earth. It gave me goose bumps just reading about it. It has made me feel safe and comfortable with God.

You and I were like that sheep, Sybil. Just bleating out our loneliness and bitterness, but all the time *He* was searching for us. And now He's carrying us home on His shoulders. What do you think of that, my friend?

Sybil: I don't know whether I know how to accept such love.

Sunlight: I've had some trouble with that, too, but I thought how foolish if the lamb had run off into the darkness when it heard the shepherd's voice and how it would have disappointed the shepherd after a night of searching.

Suppose, if sheep could talk, the sheep had said, "I'm just fine. I can take care of myself. Sorry to have caused you all the trouble," when obviously it was hungry and lost and cold, maybe even hurt. That's how dumb it would be for us to turn away from Christ, now that He has caught our attention at last.

Sybil: You misunderstand me, Meg. It's not that I *don't want* to accept that love, but I'm not sure *I can*. You see, when Bill became so immersed in his business, I nearly fell apart from hurt and loneliness. I knew if I were to survive, I simply had to steel myself against caring about anyone so much that I could be hurt. It made me cautious in all relationships, I fear, whether I want to be or not. I *want* to believe that the Good Shepherd would carry me home on His shoulders, singing—I picture Him singing, don't you?—but it's like there's a steel door in my heart that's locked and the key is lost.

Sunlight: Divorce could easily have done that to me, but I think the children were my salvation. I couldn't doubt their love. They showed it in so many ways that I never shut my heart against the world, even though I went through agony. I am going to pray, Sybil, that God will make you able to accept His love.

Now tell me what Luke said to *you.*

Sybil: First, I wanted to ask you how it went Sunday. You were magnificent on the outside, but I kept wondering how it was going inside.

Sunlight: I wish I could tell you I was all forgiveness and understanding, but the truth is I felt hate, anger, and fierce jealousy some of the time. Mostly I felt hurt. It was just hard to see them together, obviously so comfortable and content with each other. I suppose I'd always secretly hoped it wasn't working for them. But when the girls went to bed that night, they thanked me for having Jim over. Knowing how much it meant to them made it all worthwhile. It took me a long time to get to sleep, and I shed a bucket of tears, but the next time it will be easier.

Fortunately Luke took my mind off Jim this week. Michael bought me this Bible. Isn't it beautiful? What would I do without Michael?

Sybil: Learn to properly appreciate him perhaps. *(She chuckles.)* You were right. Luke is a long book, and many things in it puzzled and interested me. I was astonished at what took place in chapter 4 between Jesus and Satan in the wilderness. Somehow the devil has never been very real to me. Those pictures of him with horns and a pitchfork make him seem more like a cartoon character than anything else. Yet as I read what took place there, I had the feeling something very important was going on, that perhaps if Christ had made the slightest mismove, it might have been all up for humanity. Why do you suppose Christ would even have been tempted to kneel down and worship Satan? I can understand why He might have desired to turn the stones into bread after forty days without food, but Luke lost me on the second temptation.

Sunlight: I think I understand a little of what was involved. The whole point of Jesus' coming to this planet was to save us, I guess. Maybe to save us from Satan. So perhaps Satan was offering Him the easy way. He would *give* Him the planet if Christ would just bow to his authority. Maybe it meant Christ wouldn't have to die on the cross and suffer whatever He went through in the Garden of Gethsemane if He was willing to bow down before Satan. But it wasn't the right way, like the easy way hardly ever is. Does that make any sense?

Sybil: Yes, but how did the devil get control of this planet in the first place? If he was a troublemaker from the word *Go,* why didn't God just snuff him out?

Sunlight: I wondered that too. Those are pretty strong words in chapter 4, verse 6: "And the devil said unto him, All this power will I give thee, and the glory of them: for that is delivered unto me; and to whomsoever I will I give it." It made me uneasy to think that Satan has that much power.

Sybil: I can imagine the devil as a dangerous enemy more easily back there, but I find it hard to think of him as anything to worry about in our day. The Bible has so many stories about Christ casting out devils, but in our civilized society such things don't happen.

Sunlight: Maybe the devil just uses more sophisticated methods. Let's take the concordance in my new Bible and look up some texts about Satan, and see what we can find out. I love this system. One can learn more in twenty minutes with it than in a week of just hunting around. *(They pause as Sunlight locates "Satan" in concordance.)* It says here: "See Lucifer also" and then lists a lot of texts. I'm going to try to pick out the ones that tell where he came from and why he's here. Let's try this one: It's right in Luke where we've been studying. Chapter 10, verse 18.

Sybil: "I beheld Satan as lightning fall from heaven."

Sunlight: Well, I guess that tells us how he got here, but why? These other texts don't sound like they pertain to his origins, so let's try Lucifer. Here's one in Isaiah that sounds interesting. Where in the world is Isaiah? *(They hunt until Sybil stumbles on the book.)* Chapter 14, verse 12.

Sybil *(reads):* "How art thou fallen from heaven, O Lucifer, son of the morning! how art thou cut down to the ground, which didst weaken the nations!"

Sybil: I think it goes on about him. Do you want me to keep on reading?

Sunlight: Sure.

Sybil *(reads on):* "For thou hast said in thine heart, I will ascend into heaven, I will exalt my throne above the stars of God: I will sit also upon the mount of the congregation, in the sides of the north: I will ascend above the heights of the clouds; I will be like the most High. Yet thou shalt be brought down to hell, to the sides of the pit. They that see thee shall narrowly look upon thee, and consider thee, saying, Is this the man that made the earth to tremble, that did shake kingdoms; that made the world as a wilderness, and destroyed the cities thereof; that opened not the house of his prisoners? All the kings of the nations, even all of them, lie in glory, every one in his own house. But thou art cast out of thy grave like an abominable branch, and as the raiment of those that are slain, thrust through with a sword, that go down to the stones of the pit; as a carcase trodden under feet. Thou shalt not be joined with them in burial, because thou hast destroyed thy land, and slain thy people" [Isaiah 14:12-20].

Sunlight: Wow! What do you make of it?

Sybil: It sounds like Lucifer wanted to play God, and he got thrown out of heaven.

Sunlight: Michael taught me how to use this little strip that runs down the center of the page of my new Bible—see, you have it in yours too. If there's a small letter or number in the text you're reading, you look down the middle column until you find it. The text beside it sheds light on the one you're questioning. Isn't that fantastic? Now, here's a little *m* beside "the mount of the congregation," which sends us to Ezekiel 28:14. Let's see what that has to say. This is more exciting than *Star Wars*. *(She finds Ezekiel and reads quietly to herself.)*

Sybil: Well, come on, what does it say?

Sunlight: I'm backing up to verse 12. It seems to go with it. Sybil, I can't believe this. Lucifer must have been someone very special in heaven. Listen.

"Thus saith the Lord God; Thou sealest up the sum, full of wisdom, and perfect in beauty. Thou hast been in Eden the garden of God; every precious stone was thy covering, the sardius, topaz, and the diamond, the beryl, the onyx, and the jasper, the sapphire, the emerald, and the carbuncle, and gold: the workmanship of thy tabrets and of thy pipes was prepared in thee in the day that thou wast created. Thou art the anointed cherub that covereth; and I have set thee so: thou wast upon the holy mountain of God; thou hast walked up and down in the midst of the stones of fire.

"Thou wast perfect in thy ways from the day that thou wast created, till iniquity was found in thee. By the multitude of thy merchandise they have filled the midst of thee with violence, and thou hast sinned: therefore I will cast thee as profane out of the mountain of God: and I will destroy thee, O covering cherub, from the midst of the stones of fire. Thine heart was lifted up because of thy beauty, thou hast corrupted thy wisdom by reason of thy brightness: I will cast thee to the ground, I will lay thee before kings, that they may behold thee.

"Thou hast defiled thy sanctuaries by the multitude of thine iniquities, by the iniquity of thy traffick; therefore will I bring forth a fire from the midst of thee, it shall devour thee, and I will bring thee to ashes upon the earth in the sight of all them that behold thee. All they that know thee among the people shall be astonished at thee: thou shalt be a terror, and never shalt thou be any more" [Ezekiel 28:12-19].

Sybil: Meg, I'm speechless. How could we have never heard all this before? Lucifer must have been something indeed—beautiful, gifted, intelligent, and entrusted with some unique responsibility. But somehow he got off course *because* of his superiority, concentrating too much evidently upon his beauty and brains instead of using them. I wonder why God didn't just "think" him away and create someone else to take his place?

Sunlight: Under *Satan* I found one more text in Revelation that looks interesting. Chapter 12, verse 9. You read it.

Sybil: At least, I can find Revelation, because I know it's the last book in the Bible. Hm-m. I'll back up a few verses too. Starting with verse 7: "And there was war in heaven: Michael and his angels fought against the dragon; and the dragon fought and his angels, and prevailed not; neither was their place found any more in heaven. And the great dragon was cast out, that old serpent, called the Devil, and Satan, which deceiveth the whole world: he was cast out into the earth, and his angels were cast out with him."

That and 2 Peter 2:4 sound as if he gained the allegiance of some of the other angels. What kind of war, I wonder. A mental war, laser-beam war, war like we know it, with blood on the golden streets? But that still doesn't tell us why God allowed him to live. Obviously his troublemaking didn't stop when he arrived here on this planet.

Sunlight: The other night Jenny asked me if I would read a bit of the Bible with her before she went to sleep. I wanted her to read with me in Luke, but she was determined to start at the beginning. You know—Jen, the organized one. It had to be Genesis or nothing. So we read the first three chapters, which included the story of the serpent tempting Eve in the Garden of Eden. I noticed something there that I understand a whole lot better, now that I have a little background on the story. It's right here somewhere in the early part of Genesis 3. Yes, here it is. When Eve told the serpent that God had said they would die if they ate of the tree in the middle of the Garden, he replied, "Ye shall not surely die: for God doth know that in the day ye eat thereof, then your eyes shall be opened, and ye shall be as gods, knowing good and evil."

You see, he implied to Eve that she and Adam were living a sheltered life, that there was something mysterious and tantalizing God was keeping for His own enjoyment.

Maybe, Sybil, maybe, if God had just snuffed the devil out, all the rest of the angels would have thought Lucifer was right. That maybe evil (whatever *that* was) was something to desire. You know how people become intensely curious when they sense something we don't want them to know. So God decided to let Lucifer have a go at his own convictions, if he could find anyone to accept them. And Eve was easy prey.

Sybil: That's an interesting thought. So you think that the earth has been a sort of proving ground for the universe in which Lucifer has had freedom to demonstrate his rebellion against God. If that's the case, I'm not sure I like being a part of the experiment.

Sunlight: But I believe God didn't just back off and give Satan liberty to destroy the human race, for surely that's where it would have all ended eventually. I—I think He instead set up—what shall I call it?—an alternate system, so man had a *choice* of whom he would serve. *(Sunlight's voice rises in the excitement of her discovery.)*

In fact, I realize now that Christ's dying on the cross was the ultimate demonstration of the two systems, Sybil. Now I understand what the Crucifixion is all about. Satan's kingdom resulted in sickness, death, mental illness, and sorrow, but Christ came with His totally unselfish life, climaxing in death, to show man that *His* way offered love and safety and tenderness and healing. When He hung on the cross—even there, still concerned with men rather than Himself, while down below the very ones for whom He was dying taunted Him and ridiculed Him—the whole question of God's right to rule was settled. That kind of God I will bow to, Sybil, not just willingly but joyously, reverently, gratefully.

Sybil: Amen and amen!

Sunlight: You're laughing at me.

Sybil: No way, Meg. Just thanking God for you. You make it so clear that a child could understand it. I can see now why Satan wanted Christ to bow down to him so badly in the wilderness. He was still seeking to be like the Most High and secure his right to rule on our planet. Thank God for the victory of Jesus.

Meg, we've got to wind this up a little early tonight, because it's making me nervous having Bill shut off in the den. But I found a verse in Luke 24 that challenged me. Jesus came to some of His followers after His resurrection. They thought He was a ghost and were frightened, so He showed them His scars and let them "feel" His humanity: "Handle me, and see; for a spirit hath not flesh and bones" [verse 39]. And it says in verse 45: "Then opened he their understanding, that they might understand the scriptures." That made me realize if those men who had walked and worked with Him for three years didn't understand the

Scriptures, then probably we read them with dark glasses on ourselves. So I have been putting my finger on that text and asking God to give me understanding of the Bible too. Let's do that together tonight, for our prayer. *(They both place their fingers on the text, and Sybil prays.)*

"Dear God, open our understanding as You did so long ago for Your followers. Thank You for what You've already done for us. Let Your love be in our hearts toward all men. Amen."

Sunlight: If Bill is going to be home for a while, I think we shouldn't try to get together every week. Why don't you come to my house in a couple of weeks if it's convenient, and then we won't get together again until after the holidays. Shall we dig into the Book of John?

Sybil: Yes, I've already started reading it. Somehow tonight the things we've studied about the devil make the whole story so convincing. There's a real conflict going on in the world, and we're involved. It's a little frightening, yet exciting too. I'll call you in a couple of weeks and let you know when I can come.

Sunlight: Good night, Sybil. I'm happy for you that Bill's around. And a little envious too. *(She goes down the hall to her apartment.)*

Listening in on Sunlight and Sybil tonight brought back a lot of memories. I wish I could show her how it was, those long years ago when Lucifer roiled the peace of this land. When Sybil guessed he was a unique being, she was quite right. He was splendid indeed. We loved and trusted him, took pride in his excellence, and little realized, when he began to hint gently that perhaps God wasn't leveling with us, the rebellion and conflict that would grow out of his subtle warfare. By the time he'd finished, he'd convinced a third of the angels [Revelation 12:4] that God was unjust in His dealings with us. I think by the time they were cast out they well knew they had made a grave mistake, but they would not turn back. We had not known the meaning of the word *sorrow* until that day. Oh, the emptiness of heaven! We had lost loved friends and a deeply respected leader. I'm sure that some minds had doubts as to the justice of what had taken place. I'll admit, I myself wondered if Lucifer could possibly be right in his accusations, but as I had watched the reign of the Prince through eons of time, I had seen nothing but love and fairness in all His dealings, and I decided to cast my lot with Him, rather than trust to Lucifer with his inflammatory teachings. Oh, how many times I have been thankful for that decision as I have watched the tears and pain of earth-life unfold before my eyes! That which God withheld from us, we were well off not to know.

Things are going too well for Sybil and Sunlight. The Rebel does not let go of his citizens so easily. What plottings lurk in his crafty mind?

I have noted the young man Michael searching furiously in his Bible this week, a can of beer ever beside him on the table. He has been making careful notes. Sunlight will be astonished at the conclusion to which he has come.

Here in the Peaceful Kingdom angels have been coming and going with a new urgency, and Earth Friend is beginning to release His power upon humans with stronger impact. Many on earth, I have noted, are beginning to open their Bibles with searching hearts. They are quickly making discoveries that once took others a lifetime. With the aid of Earth Friend, Sunlight and Sybil grasp things so quickly. There is an undertone of excitement in this place.

On earth trouble reigns, with more to come. The Prince will soon release those angels whose special assignment it is to hold back the winds of strife [Revelation 7:1] from their task. It is a grave hour in the universe.

I can't get Lucifer out of my mind. You know, sometimes, up until the cross, I looked with pity upon him and his followers. I longed to have things as they were before, to see him reinstated, to have access once more to his vibrant personality, his talents, his challenging mind. I wondered, if he were given another chance, that perhaps all could be as it had been before. But that awful day when the Prince hung on the cross, even the night before as He agonized in the Garden, I saw the fury with which Lucifer sought to destroy Him. Finally I understood the evil within that once-glorious being. I knew there could be no turning back, and I have not found it in my heart to pity him since that day.

Chapter Seven

The Rebel's attack was more cruel than I could have anticipated. My heart is too heavy to record my observations on the following scene.

(In Sunlight's living room. Everything is in a state of confusion, with Sunlight weeping, Jim sitting with head in hands, and Carol, white and silent, in chair by herself.)

Jim: We have to pull ourselves together, Meg, and do whatever it is people do at such times. Do you want a funeral or just something quick and quiet?

Sunlight: I could never bear that long-drawn-out process in which one stands around and greets people. Jim, I don't think I can go through any of it.

Carol: Don't cry, Mom. *(She goes to her mother and puts her arms around her.)* You still have me.

Sunlight: Carol, tell me carefully again what happened.

Carol: It was just like I said, Mommy. We got off the school bus at the corner, and Jen ran out to cross the street. She must not have looked, and there was a car turning onto our street. I heard the brakes squeal and Jen scream, then she was lying in the street and people were all around. A policeman brought me here and called Daddy. That's all. She can't be dead, Mom. Are they sure? I made the policeman wait while I picked up her books and stuff 'cause I thought she'd be home later. Jen's fussy about having her homework done, and she'd hate having her books get wet.

Jim *(taking Carol onto his lap):*   Jen would have appreciated that, Button. You did everything just right. You mustn't mind if your mom and I cry. We hurt so bad inside that we *have* to cry. Maybe you need to cry too. Let's just sit here for a few minutes and comfort each other, then maybe you could stay with Sybil for a little while so your mom and I can go out and take care of the things that have to be done.

(A few moments later Sunlight and Jim, Carol between them, knock at Sybil's door. She responds, a bit startled to find them together there.)

Sybil: Well, Meg, Jim, do come in. What brings you? *(Then, noting their faces, she pales.)* Something awful has happened. I'm afraid to ask.

Sunlight *(quietly):*   Jen has been killed in an accident, Sybil. Just a few hours ago when she got out of school. We're still in a state of shock, I guess, but we have to go to the hospital and take care of things. We wondered if you would keep Carol for a bit until we get back?

Sybil *(her eyes full of tears):*   Oh, you poor children! How terrible! Of course, Carol may stay. What else can I do for you? *(She places her arms around Sunlight and holds her tightly for a moment.)*

Jim: I don't think there's a thing, but thanks for offering. We're going to have a little private service day after tomorrow, and I think Meg would like it if you and Bill would come. Her parents are clear across the country, and she doesn't want them to make the long trip.

(Sunlight bends down to hug Carol good-bye but cannot speak further to Sybil.)

A month has passed. Nothing marks the spot where a golden-haired ten-year-old stepped from a school bus to her death. Traffic ebbs and flows, pedestrians have ceased already to point out the scene of the accident, her schoolmates no longer whisper nervously about the tragedy. Life just flows over the place where a little girl once stood, until it seems perhaps one only dreamed she had been there at all. That's the way earthlings handle death. I suppose it's the only way they can, and still survive. It's been easier for Jim because he was used to living without the child, but Sunlight is walking the dark valley alone. She has canceled her Bible study with Sybil. In fact, she has cut herself off from all contact with her fellow humans. My heart aches for little Carol. Usually so vibrant and alive, she has become quiet and introspective, with dark circles beneath her great brown eyes. Sybil, in her wise maturity, has refused to let Sunlight turn her away and is now sitting in Sunlight's kitchen.

Sybil: I sent Carol down to watch TV with Bill because I wanted to talk with you, Meg. You can't go on like this, shutting yourself away from everyone. It's no good for Carol. She looks terrible. I'm not going to say I know how awful you feel, because I don't. I never had a child. I know it must be agony, and especially so because you and Jen were closer, living here without Jim. But we have to go on, Meg, no matter how much we hurt. For Carol's sake you must smile again and have your friends in. She misses Michael. That was a pretty tough experience for a seven-year-old, and I fear she dwells on it too much. Don't forget, my friend, that little girl is lonely too. You need each other. I wanted to share something with you I read in the Bible the other day. I copied it down.

Sunlight: I don't want to hear it, Sybil. Where was our loving, compassionate God when Jen got off that bus?

Sybil: The same place He was when His *own* Son hung on the cross, Meg. Just waiting for this whole long drama to finalize. There's never been any assurance that those who follow Him will escape tragedy—only that they will have strength to bear it. God Himself didn't escape tragedy, so how can we expect to?

Sunlight: I don't want any part of a conflict in which innocent children get caught in the warfare.

Sybil: I doubt God wants any part of it either—He didn't create little children to die but to laugh and play and bring joy to their parents. But as long as the devil has freedom on this planet, I fear innocent children *will die*. If we trust Christ, as these people did who pleased Him so much when He was here, then Jen's death doesn't have to be a tragedy.

Sunlight *(sharply):*   Well, it's a tragedy for me. I appreciate your concern, Sybil, but I don't think you can begin to understand what I'm going through. Thanks for being so great to Carol. She looks forward to her little visit with you and Bill every afternoon. But I'll have to work this thing out in my own way. Right now, it's all I can do to function. When little girls come laughing into the store after school in the afternoons I get sick at my stomach. I'm not sure I know how to handle it, Sybil, or that I can ever feel the same about God again. You'll have to accept that. Come visit if you like, but don't talk to me about God.

Sybil: If that's how you want it, Meg, but I think you need God more now than ever before. *(She rises to leave but doesn't take up the slip of paper on which she has written the Bible verse. When she has gone, Sunlight picks it up.)*

   "For the enemy hath persecuted my soul; he hath smitten my life down to the ground; he hath made me to dwell in darkness, as those that have been long dead. Therefore is my spirit overwhelmed within me; my heart within me is desolate." *(Tears stream down Sunlight's face.)*

   "I remember the days of old; I meditate on all thy

works, I muse on the works of thy hands. I stretch forth my hands unto thee: my soul thirsteth after thee, as a thirsty land. Selah. Hear me speedily, O Lord: my spirit faileth: hide not thy face from me, lest I be like unto them that go down into the pit. Cause me to hear thy lovingkindness in the morning; for in thee do I trust: cause me to know the way wherein I should walk; for I lift up my soul unto thee.''

(Sunlight puts her head on the table and sobs, then places the piece of paper in her Bible and goes about supper preparations. Hours later as she lies in bed, trying to sleep, Carol comes into her room.)

Sunlight: What are you doing up? You should have been asleep hours ago.

Carol: I can't sleep, Mom. It's so lonely in there without Jen. Whenever I look at her empty bed I feel all sick inside, and when I'm dropping off to sleep I see her lying in the street with dirty snow in her hair and on her blue jacket. And I see her hand, Mom, holding that new pen Daddy gave her for her birthday. Her hand was OK, and I was sure she was all right. But I could never look at the other side of her where the car hit, because I was afraid to see her face, like maybe her face wouldn't be OK. Oh, Mom, it was awful. *(Carol crawls onto Sunlight's bed, sobbing. They hold each other, crying softly.)*

Carol: Where is she now, Mom?

Sunlight: In a vault, waiting for springtime when the ground will be thawed so she can be buried. You know. I told you that.

Carol: I mean where is she *really?* A girl at school told me she's in heaven, alive and happy, but I thought if that were true, you would have told me, and you wouldn't cry all the time.

Sunlight: Carol, I don't know the answer to that question. Many people think you go straight to heaven when you die, if you're good enough to go, that is, but something Sybil and I read in the Bible makes me wonder.

Carol: You told us once the Bible answered the questions about where we came from and where we are going. Why don't you look now and see what it says. If Jen is up in heaven with God, it's silly for us to be crying. Turn on the light, Mom, and look. Please.

Sunlight: Carol, it's not that simple. The Bible is not always easy to decipher. You have to study and search for the answers sometimes. Anyhow, I feel angry with God and don't know that I want to read the Bible anymore.

Carol (her eyes wide with amazement): Angry with God? He didn't kill Jen, Mom. You told us yourself that God is loving and kind.

Sunlight: I don't want to talk about it, Carol. You may stay here in my bed tonight if you like. Maybe we'll both sleep better.

Carol: I want to know what the Bible says before I go to sleep. Can't you use that thing in the back of the Bible, like Michael showed you? Just look up *death* or *dead*.

Sunlight: Carol, I told you I don't wish to read the Bible right now. Go to sleep. We both have to get up early in the morning.

Carol: You go to sleep if you want to, Mom, but I'm going to see if I can figure out where Jen is. How do you spell *death*? (She gets out of bed and takes Meg's Bible from the bedside stand.)

Sunlight (sighing and switching on the light): Where did you get this stubborn streak of yours? If it were over anything else, I'd tan your fanny, but I guess if you need to know, you need to know. We may not learn a thing, you understand. I fear the world has been haggling over where the dead are for centuries, so it's expecting quite a bit for you and me to solve the mystery tonight. I'll run down through *death* and *dead,* and if I find anything that looks enlightening, we'll check it out *(she flips to the Book of Psalms and reads)*: "The dead praise not the Lord, neither any that go down into silence" [Psalm 115:17].

Carol: That doesn't sound like they are up in heaven.

Sunlight: All right, here's another: "For the living know that they shall die: *but the dead know not any thing, neither have they any more a reward; for the memory of them is forgotten. Also their love, and their hatred, and their envy, is now perished;* neither have they any more a portion for ever in any thing that is done under the sun" [Ecclesiastes 9:5, 6].

Carol: Mom, you know, that's perfectly clear. See, the Bible isn't hard. Now find another.

(Sunlight looks up two or three texts but finds nothing relating to the actual state of death.)

Sunlight: I'm just going to try a couple more, Carol. Here's another one in Ecclesiastes 9: "Whatsoever thy hand findeth to do, do it with thy might; *for there is no work, nor device, nor knowledge, nor wisdom, in the grave, whither thou goest.*"

Carol: Where do people get the idea Jen's up in heaven? I guess I'd like her to be there, but she isn't.

Sunlight: Maybe you'll like this one better. It has a happier sound. "Thy dead men shall live, together with my dead body shall they arise. Awake and sing, ye that dwell in dust: for thy dew is as the dew of herbs, and the earth shall cast out the dead" [Isaiah 26:19].

Carol: Will it really happen, Mom? Will God really raise people from the dead?

Sunlight: Yes, Button, He will, because He has already raised some people. Let me show you something Sybil and I ran into in our study of Matthew *(she turns to the account of Christ's death in Matthew 27 and reads):*

"And the graves were opened; and many bodies of the saints which slept arose, and came out of the graves after his resurrection, and went into the holy city, and appeared unto many" [verses 52, 53].

Well, one more text: "For the Lord himself shall descend from heaven with a shout, with the voice of the archangel, and with the trump of God: and the dead in Christ shall rise first: then we which are alive and remain shall be caught up together with them in the clouds, to meet the Lord in the air: and so shall we ever be with the Lord. Wherefore comfort one another with these words" [1 Thessalonians 4:16-18].

Carol: Did you hear that, Mom? When Jesus comes, He's going to really wake up the dead, and then He'll take the rest of us up with them to heaven. That means you and I and Jen will all go to heaven together. I almost like that better than her getting there ahead of us. We could all see it for the first time together. And Sybil and Bill, and Daddy and Marie, and Michael.

Sunlight: Slow down, Sweetheart. Not *everyone* will go to heaven, I fear. Only those who truly love Jesus and accept what He did for them when He hung on the cross.

Carol *(quietly):* Jen loved Him. One night after we got into bed she told me that since she began reading her Bible she could go to sleep better at night. She used to put it under her pillow. Before, she would cry a lot about you and Daddy, and she made me swear not to tell, but after she read the Bible, she said the hole in her heart was filling up with Jesus' love.

Sunlight: Oh, Carol, thank you for telling me that. I think maybe you knew Jen better than any of us. And thank you for making me look up all those texts. That last one filled my heart with hope. Now you and I must be sure that *we* are ready when Jesus comes, so that we can meet Jen and all go up into the clouds together. It seems almost like a fairy tale, doesn't it?

Carol: Except that we read it right in the Bible, and there are no fairy tales in the Bible. I feel OK inside for the first time since Jen died. Let's go to sleep.

(They turn out the light and curl up together in Sunlight's bed.)

Carol *(sleepily):* Are you still mad at God, Mom?

Sunlight: *No,* Button, thanks to you, I guess I have my head on straight.

And thanks to Carol, I can breathe again. I have trembled for Sunlight as I watched the Rebel attempt to smother her in a cloud of doubt and bitterness. I realized she was literally staggering with sorrow and, of course, that's when the Rebel and his troops move in. So I wondered how Earth Friend would break through to her heart, especially when Michael and Sybil failed to reach her. But in His infinite wisdom, Earth Friend knew the little one could touch that mother's heart as could no other.

The Prince came by a few minutes ago, and I started to tell Him the good news, but He just smiled at me and said, "I know, Jared, I know." Sometimes I forget He knows about them all, moment by moment, like they're engraved on the palms of His hands.

Chapter Eight

(Jim comes for Carol, but she is at Sybil's apartment, so he chats with Sunlight for a few moments before picking her up.)

Jim: How are you doing, Meg? I've tried to keep busy day and night so I wouldn't think about Jen, and I know it's been easier on me than you, but even so, these weeks have been rough. I wake up in the night, and it hits me all over again like it happened yesterday, and I just lie there wrestling with it for hours. These things happen to other people's kids, but not to our Jen. Marie tries to understand, but I guess a person can't when it's not her own.

Sunlight: I never dreamed such pain existed. I thought when you left that nothing could ever hurt that bad again, but this has been worse. She was so young—all her life before her. But there's no point in talking about it. It has happened, and we must go on. Carol is great company to me, and I'm learning to lean on God—at least part of the time.

Jim: I never realized until this happened what it's like to lose someone. It made me understand what a wretched thing I've done to you. I've said I was sorry a good many times, Meg, not really comprehending what I'd put you through. Now I want to say it one more time with a new knowledge that no words, however sincere, can begin to touch the problem.

Sunlight: Let's discuss this once more and then forget it forever. I did hurt terribly, Jim, because I loved you so much. I still do love you, but I'm no longer bitter. No thanks to me. I learned from Jesus Christ that only pride keeps one bitter, and He took that pride from me. *I forgive you.* I say those words only because you may need to hear them so that you can go on with your life, free of guilt. Now, please, let's never discuss it again. Here's Carol's jacket. Don't forget she has school tomorrow and needs to be home early.

Jim: You know, you're some girl, Meg. We'd like you and Carol to come for dinner next Sunday. Bring Michael if you'd like.

(Jim goes down the hall to collect Carol, and Sybil soon arrives at Sunlight's apartment, Bible in hand.)

Sybil: Well, it's been a long time, Meg. I've been plugging away at this stuff all by myself, and I missed you.

Sunlight: I guess I'd never have gotten myself together if Carol hadn't forced me to check the whereabouts of the dead that night. Somehow the sight of her standing there in her nightie, Bible in hand, so determined to find out about Jen, just broke my heart. I *had* to help her.

Sybil: Bill and I love that child. Meg, because of the long time lapse, I guess I've studied John more thoroughly than any of the other Gospels. In fact, I went further on into the New Testament. Have you felt like reading at all?

Sunlight: Not until Carol got me started, but then I found such comfort in that one text I told you about in 1 Thessalonians 4 that I have been digging away furiously ever since. I have to know *everything,* Sybil.

Sybil: It seemed to me when I finished John that I *did* know everything, or at least enough so that my head was swimming. I came to the conclusion that anyone going all the way with this business needed two baptisms, one in the water and one by the Holy Spirit [John 1:26-34]. I wouldn't know where to start getting either one.

Sunlight: I thought about that, too, but I'm not quite sure

I'm ready for that yet. When the time comes, I want to be baptized right down in the water, just as Jesus was. I can't believe sprinkling suffices. There must be some deep significance to being immersed in the water like that. Maybe the baptism in water signifies our commitment to Christ and our acceptance of His sacrifice and then the baptism of the Holy Spirit enables us to live for Him afterward. I found a verse in Acts that determines who receives the Holy Spirit. Before we started this study, all I knew about religion was what I read in the newspaper or in an occasional *Time* or *Newsweek*. But I do know some have been stressing that we receive the Holy Spirit. So when I saw a text about having the Holy Spirit, I underlined it in my Bible. Here it is.

"And we are his witnesses of these things; and so is also the Holy Ghost, *whom God hath given to them that obey him*" [Acts 5:32].

Sybil: So unless one is living according to all that he knows, he could well miss the gift of the Holy Spirit.

Sunlight: I think it is more than that. It's not just the light that he has but also what he might have had, had he opened his Bible and studied.

Sybil: Meg, I noted that John used the word *believe* over and over again. It brings us right back to the matter of faith that we discovered in our very first study. I wonder what it really means to "believe" on Christ.

(Sunlight answers a knock at the door to find Michael. She invites him in.)

Michael: Sorry to interrupt you two, but I had something I wanted to share with Meg. I'm glad you're here, too, Sybil. I guess we're all in this together.

Sunlight: Well, what is it? It's got to be important to bring you on a Sunday afternoon when there's football on television. Out with it.

Michael: No, I want you to go on with whatever you were discussing, and when you finish, I'll spring my discovery. *(He chuckles.)* If I have any profound thoughts as you go along, I'll toss them in.

Sybil: We are talking about the Book of John and how much emphasis John puts on belief, and we wondered what it really means to believe. A long time ago we decided that at least it would prompt us to search to grasp all there is to know about Him, to spend time with Him. But is there more?

Sunlight: It's the strangest thing, but lately, every time I pick up my Bible to study, I feel troubled about the cigarette I have in my hand. I don't think there's anything in the Bible that says not to smoke or drink, yet somehow I don't feel comfortable doing either of those things anymore.

Michael: I think I know why you may feel that way. Both habits are self-destructive, which hardly seems compatible with God's desire for us to be healthy and happy. You've always smoked far too much, Meg. Why don't you back off?

Sunlight: Well, I only brought it up, thinking that perhaps as we grow closer to God, He makes us aware of those things in our lives which disturb Him. Then *believing* expands to encompass obedience and—I guess the word would be *submission.* So believing could turn out to be quite an assignment. And as for your suggestion, Michael, I've *tried* to quit smoking. One hour leaves me climbing the walls.

Michael: I haven't felt very comfortable in a bar lately either. I just quit going but find the beer in my own refrigerator a tougher foe.

Sybil: Are you sure *believing* is as complicated as all that?

Michael: I think the act of accepting Jesus Christ as one's Saviour is our entry into eternal life. He has paid for our sins. It's as simple as that. But by that choice on my part, I have become what Scripture calls a son of God, and how can a son of God walk down the street puffing on a cigarette or idle away an evening at the bar? It's like trying to imagine the apostle Paul addressing the Greeks with a cigar in one hand. Let's be honest with ourselves. We know that such habits aren't good for us. If Someone has valued me enough to die for me, to adopt me into His family just as I am, then simple loving gratitude compels me to reflect His values, His family traditions. That isn't what *made me* a member of His family—His death did that, no strings attached—but *my love for Him* compels me. To say nothing of the fact that His life-style aims for my ultimate happiness, in contrast to the inherent destructiveness of my previous ways.

Sunlight: Michael, you made it so beautiful that it makes me want to be free of cigarettes forever. Now I see it as something I can do for Him, like a gift. But—but I *can't* do it.

Michael: I'm sorry, I don't have the answer to that one, but there has to be one. God doesn't ask the impossible. Let's just take it one day at a time and see where He leads.

Sunlight *(her face aglow, excitedly clasping her hands in her lap):* There was a portion of chapter 12 in John that I especially loved. Jesus is speaking, and it's just a little while before His death. He says in verse 24, "Except a corn of wheat fall into the ground and die, it abideth alone: but if it die, it bringeth forth much fruit."

I know He was talking about His soon-coming death and what it would mean to humanity, but I had the feeling He was saying we, too, must experience some kind of death. That if we were willing, the results of that death would be as exciting as a shoot of green corn coming up out of the ground. Somehow I expect this "death" takes courage—enough courage to trust that out of the death experience will come something infinitely better than what we call life now. Do I have you thoroughly confused?

Sybil *(laughing happily):* Maybe this death means turning over every corner of our being to Him. Our thoughts and our ambitions, our motives and our decisions. I have a feeling letting go of our lives to such an extent would be a kind of death.

Sunlight: I think I may know what you mean. Like maybe I would say to Him, "It's OK about Jen's accident. I know You love her and me and that You make no mistakes," instead of going around and around in my mind trying to find a reason.

Michael: God didn't kill Jenny, you know.

Sunlight: No, but He could have prevented it. And considering her brief exposure to Him, He couldn't have found a more loyal little friend.

Sybil: Maybe that's why He didn't step in, Meg. All was well between Him and Jen. If He interfered in all Satan's plans, it wouldn't be much of an experiment. He has to allow the devil some freedom for his ugly demonstration. No one would ever know what he was like if God didn't let him do anything. And He trusted you to hold steady, Meg. I know it sounds easy to say that, but I can't see any other way that would really expose the devil for what he is.

Sunlight: Well, I almost failed the test. It was Carol who held steady. But I want you both to look at John 12, verses 27 and 28. There is something so human about Jesus here that that—that I long to reach out and touch Him. He's saying, "Now is my soul troubled; and what shall I say? Father, save me from this hour: but for this cause came I unto this hour. Father, glorify thy name."

It made me realize that Christ actually wrestled with the issue of dying for us. And then submitted to His assignment. It wasn't just play-acting, some sort of ritual He went through.

Sybil: I see what you mean. We always tend to think of Him as Mr. Magic in a human body, but the more I study, the more I sense that the only part of Him different from us was that He wrestled with His Father on His knees, day by day. Which, of course, I believe holds a crucial message for us. But if you want to get a clearer picture of His struggle, go back to Mark's description of Christ in the Garden of Gethsemane. I'll read it to you.

"And they came to a place which was named Gethsemane: and he saith to his disciples, Sit ye here, while I shall pray. And he taketh with him Peter and James and John, and began to be sore amazed, and to be very heavy; and saith unto them, My soul is exceeding sorrowful unto death; tarry ye here, and watch. And he went forward a little, and fell on the ground, and prayed that, if it were possible, the hour might pass from him. And he said, Abba, Father, all things are possible unto thee; take away this cup from me: nevertheless not what I will, but what thou wilt" [Mark 14:32-36].

I fear we know nothing of what took place during that hour. I cannot read Christ's cry on the cross, "My God, my God, why hast thou forsaken me?" without tears. I don't begin to grasp what was involved, but I believe He felt the possibility of losing everything there in that blackness. Yet, even under those conditions, He did not reject the cross. It's more than the human mind can absorb, I fear. At least mine.

Sunlight: Michael, I want to know what you came here to tell us.

Michael: I warn you, it's startling news, and I have no idea whether you are ready for it or not. Ever since that night when you asked me to read those chapters to you, Meg,

I've been searching. That account of the Crucifixion met some need that had been aching inside me for years, and I made up my mind if the Bible had the answer to the world's questions, I was going to dig them out.

In my search I ran across many references to the Sabbath. It seemed that in the Gospels, Christ was always attempting to improve the quality of Sabbathkeeping. I was aware, as I told you, that the Sabbath referred to in the Old Testament and in Christ's lifetime was the seventh-day Sabbath of the Jews. Saturday as we know it today. I went back and studied its origins in Genesis [2, 3] and traced its history on through the Bible. Then I began the search for the text in which Christ established Sunday as the day of worship in honor of His resurrection. I used the best concordance I could get my hands on and came up with nothing. The first day of the week is mentioned a few times, but not in any significant way. It gave me an eerie feeling, for I had been so sure it would be there, simple and obvious.

You remember Joe Wescott, Maggie? Well, he's a minister now. He has the West Avenue Lutheran Church. I decided to give him a call and let him straighten me out. He was tickled to hear from me. Said he'd lost all contact with most of the old high school crowd and insisted I come over for the evening. After we had a little polite chitchat about old times, I came right to the point. We were sitting in his study with our Bibles, and I was waiting for him to open his and show me the elusive text. But instead he just sat there looking a little embarrassed and amused. And then he said, "I hate to disappoint you, Mike, but you aren't going to find the text you're looking for. It just isn't there."

I will never forget that moment. Millions of Christians over the years going faithfully to church every Sunday with no Biblical basis. I must have looked as astonished as I felt, for Joe chuckled. He said there is not even any Biblical record of the disciples making a change after Christ's death. To the contrary, he showed me several texts that indicated they simply kept on observing the seventh-day Sabbath as before [Acts 13:14; 16:13; 17:2; 18:4].

Eventually, however, Christians began keeping Saturday and Sunday side by side—Saturday in deference to God's original command and Sunday as a sort of festival day in honor of Christ's resurrection. Joe pointed out that this festival day did not result from any divine command.

Several factors evidently had bearings upon the gradual shift from the seventh day to the first. Because of various revolts in the second century, the Jews became unpopular, and it was more comfortable to avoid all identification with them—the Sabbath, of course, being one of the more obvious Jewish observances.

Also, because many Christians fasted on the Sabbath, another rule of their own making, it seemed a rather austere day in comparison with the festivities of Sunday. Human nature being what it is, they naturally preferred eating and singing to fasting and meditating.

Sybil: Michael, are you trying to tell us that Jesus Christ expects us to observe Saturday as the Sabbath?

Sunlight: Let's hear him out, Sybil.

Michael: I know it's long and a bit heavy, but it's also exciting. In the fourth century Constantine the Great came along and smiled on Christianity. No more persecution. Sigh of relief for the Christians. He instituted the venerable Day of the Sun (Sunday) as an official *rest* day in which all workshops were to be closed and the citizens of the realm were to relax. By the sixth century the shift from Sabbath to Sunday worship was almost universal, yet Joe said there have been those in every age who observed the seventh day as God originally commanded. And he added that they usually brought persecution upon themselves as a result.

Joe also commented that the Catholics have had their own little chuckle at Protestants since the Reformation. An opponent of Luther's named Eck once wrote *(Michael takes a small notebook from his pocket):* "The Scripture teaches: Remember that you keep holy the Sabbath day. . . . Yet the church has changed the Sabbath to the Lord's day by its own authority, upon which you have no Scripture" (translated from Johann Eck, *Enchiridion Locorum Communium . . . Adversus Lutheranos* [*Handbook of Commonplaces Against the Lutherans*], 1533 ed.).

He gave me another quote from the June 11, 1950, issue of a Catholic publication: *Our Sunday Visitor:* "In all their official books of instruction Protestants claim that their religion is based on the Bible, and the Bible only, and they reject tradition as even a part of their rule of faith. . . .

"There is no place in the New Testament where it is distinctly stated that Christ changed the day of worship from Saturday to Sunday. Yet all Protestants . . . observe the Sunday; Protestants follow *tradition* in observing the Sunday."

Sunlight: Why did Joe have all this material at his fingertips?

Michael: He has a bulging file on the subject and a very uneasy mind.

Sunlight: You mean he believes the seventh day is the Sabbath, Michael? Then why isn't he preaching it from the pulpit?

Michael: It takes courage, Maggie. He'd probably soon be out of a job. Truth that demands change is seldom popular. But he's doing a lot of thinking and is thrilled to find someone else who isn't just walking unquestioningly with the crowd. I told him about you two, and he confided that he had a handful in his congregation who were opening their Bibles with a real thirst to know God.

Sybil: But what's the point to all of this? What difference does it make? How would it change our lives, should we decide to make the switch?

Michael: Well, Joe says the Sabbath was intended to be a time in which man would put everything secular or distracting aside and enjoy companionship with his Maker [Exodus 20:8-11; Isaiah 58:13, 14]. He says there are those today who observe it in just that way, refraining from secular work, worshiping and fellowshiping together, ministering to those about them in ways for which they might not have time during the week.

Sunlight *(silent for a moment):* I think I have to search out what the Bible has to say myself before I can make a decision like that. Would Joe lend you his file for a few days so that we can study his findings? *(She glances at him intently.)* You're convinced already, aren't you, Michael?

Michael *(nodding slowly):* Beyond a shadow of a doubt. In fact I've already kept my first Sabbath.

Sybil *(looking surprised):* What did you do?

Michael: I spent the morning studying my Bible and praying, and in the afternoon I went with Joe to the hospital. He uses Sabbath to minister to the sick. It's his way of observing the day without rocking any boats.

Sunlight: Jim will be bringing Carol soon, but before we close the Book of John, I'd like us all to turn to chapter 6, verses 66-69. *(She reads the scriptures to the others.)*

"From that time many of his disciples went back, and walked no more with him. Then said Jesus unto the twelve, Will ye also go away? Then Simon Peter answered him, Lord, to whom shall we go? thou hast the words of eternal life. And we believe *and are sure* that thou art that Christ, the Son of the living God."

> Michael, do you believe, and are you sure, that He was the Christ, Son of the living God?

Michael: I do.

Sunlight: Sybil, do you believe, and are you sure, that He was the Christ, the Son of the living God?

Sybil *(hesitating for a moment):* I do.

Sunlight: And I, too, believe and am sure. If I read my Bible correctly, in this sober declaration of our faith we have just received the gift of salvation. Can it be as simple as that?

Michael: I think that's why it's hard for people. It's so simple that we cannot grasp it. Few gifts are given on this earth that we haven't earned, one way or another. We don't even really know how to receive anything small, much less forgiveness for our ugly lives.

Sybil: I think our believing must also include acceptance of His power to save and a response on our part.

Michael: Surely Simon Peter included all that in his statement of dedication, but I'm glad you defined it for us.

Sunlight: Will you pray, Michael?

Michael: We have just made a commitment to You, Lord. In accepting You as the Christ, we take on whatever that involves, joyously, willingly, knowing You have nothing but our happiness in mind. Please guide us in our future study. Amen.

Michael has made an exciting discovery, for the Sabbath is, and always has been, an issue in the struggle between the Prince and Lucifer. Just as the tree in the Garden of Eden was a test to Adam and Eve, so this matter of the Sabbath is a test to Adam's descendants.

So cleverly has Lucifer shrouded its importance that few have caught it, though the Bible clearly witnesses to it.

The Rebel will batter Sunlight and her friends unmercifully, has even now led Sunlight down the rockiest path of her young and troubled life, but if they fall on their knees and wrench from the Scriptures all that is there for them, he will have no success. Already, Earth Friend is flooding their minds with understanding, just as He is pursuing each earthling with a final, driven intensity.

The mighty angel of Revelation 18:1 is even now shedding his glory over the earth, providing a last chance for lost humans. His message, "Babylon the great is fallen, is fallen, and is become the habitation of devils, and the hold of every foul spirit, and a cage of every unclean and hateful bird," is a sober one indeed. Babylon represents every evil program and movement and erroneous religion that the Rebel has created over the centuries. The cup of iniquity is nearly full. Time is running out for the earth.

The mighty angel pleads with humanity, "Come out of her, my people, that ye be not partakers of her sins, and that ye receive not of her plagues" [Revelation 18:4], and this should drive men to their knees. It is really the cry of the Prince to His followers all across the earth, a heart-wrenching cry to those for whom He died—COME OUT OF HER, MY PEOPLE. Come out before it is too late. Forsake the bars, the television sets, the social causes that neglect men's souls, the churches where there is enthusiasm but not truth. Put aside the toys of earth: the yachts, the town houses, the stereos, the jets whisking men from sea to sea. Take your Bibles and search as though your life was at stake. For it is. "Ye shall seek me, and find me," the Prince says, "when ye shall search for me with all your heart." Now is the hour.

I see the accelerating pace all about me here in the Peaceful Kingdom. There will be some breathtaking events to record, and then this journal will be closed forever.

Chapter Nine

(The long winter months have passed. Sun-warmed waves splash jauntily against Rochester's wharves, and the city's citizens walk with quick and eager steps into springtime. Michael and his friend Joe Wescott, a tall, craggy, dark-haired young man, are seated in Sunlight's living room.)

Joe: I need to talk with you and Michael, Meg. You know, Michael and I have been doing a lot of studying together these past months, and it's getting harder and harder for me to preach on a day that I don't consider the Sabbath. I know Michael has shared with you some of the things we've discussed about what will happen to our world. I find most of my congregation isn't ready to hear them. They want a good-neighbor kind of gospel that may have been fine a few years ago, but time is running out, and I feel the need to speak to them of sober things. I am coming to an impasse in my life in which I must make some choices. I can procrastinate no longer. If Jean were with me in this, I wouldn't hesitate for a moment, but she's alarmed and bitter that my study has led me to this place.

Sunlight: What will happen if you share your convictions on the Sabbath with your congregation?

Joe: I expect I will have preached my last sermon. Do you have any idea what it means to walk away from a group of people you have loved and nurtured for five years?

Sunlight: No, but I do know how it feels to hurt. What would you do then?

Michael: There's a counseling position open in the department at work. I think they will count Joe a real find. We're behind you, Joe, if you feel the time has come.

(Joe sits with head in hands, sorrow permeating his entire being.)

Sunlight: Joe, perhaps you're wrestling too much with this. If God has led you into new areas of truth, it is a time for rejoicing. Share it with your people. Some will believe, and the others must move ahead in their own way and at their own pace. Even Christ had to accept such compromise. Prepare your sermon, and Michael and I will pray for you. Next Sunday we will be in your congregation backing you with our love.

Joe *(looking up and smiling):* Thank you, Meg. I needed that. Of course you're right. I've never known such joy as these past few months since Michael and I have studied together. My heart had hungered for someone who was searching as I was. I feel the Holy Spirit has revealed truth to us in a remarkable way. That is, indeed, cause for rejoicing. *I will do it.* Next Sunday. Promise me you will both pray as never before that I will make truth clear to my people.

Michael: You know we will, Joe. *(The men leave, and Sunlight kneels beside her chair.)*

(One week later Michael and Sunlight are seated in the hushed stillness of Joe Wescott's church. They look at Joe's wife, Jean, and his two children a few pews ahead and wonder if she is aware of his plan.)

Sunlight *(whispering):* I'm scared to death for him.

Michael: He'll be OK. Just pray. Christ did some pretty scary things for us.

(Joe stands in the pulpit, his face paler than usual against the darkness of his unruly hair.)

Joe: I have come to you this morning, my people, with a solemn message. I would like to ask that you put from your minds the cares of your personal lives, the mundane events flitting too easily in and out of our thoughts. I ask for your full attention, for when you leave this place, you must make a decision. As your pastor, I have not, unfortunately perhaps, asked many decisions of you, but today is an exception.

I have been searching my Bible as never before. I feel we are right upon the borders of those climactic events that will bring the history of this planet to a close. It is not a time for planning church bazaars. It is a time to search our souls.

Ever since my seminary days I have pondered the matter of Saturday versus Sunday as the Sabbath. . . .

(Joe speaks eloquently upon the historical back-ground of the Sabbath and then moves into those Biblical passages relating to it. Michael and Sunlight pray fervently and observe the stoical faces of Joe's congregation. Only the occasional fretting of a weary child breaks the utter stillness. Finally he brings his plea, for that's what it must be, to a tender close.)

Joe: Beloved, the Sabbath is a meaningful gift from our Creator-God. He considered it so important He placed it in the very heart of His Ten Commandments [Exodus 20:8-11]. The other commandments dealt with practical matters. They were good commonsense rules that are as obviously necessary to us today as then—but at first glance the Sabbath commandment appears to have no practical purpose. It is rather to maintain man's joy in his God. It is a love day between Creator and creature. God reminds His people of His supreme power as *Creator* in the closing words of that fourth commandment: "For in six days the Lord made heaven and earth, the sea, and all that in them is, and rested the seventh day: wherefore the Lord blessed the sabbath day, and hallowed it."

Please turn with me, my brothers and sisters, as I close, to Revelation 14:6 and 7. This angel that John describes has a message for the last generation before Christ returns, and again we find the warning to worship the *Creator*.

"And I saw another angel fly in the midst of heaven, having the everlasting gospel to preach unto them that dwell on the earth, and to every nation, and kindred, and tongue, and people, saying with a loud voice, *Fear God, and give glory to him; for the hour of his judgment is come: and worship him that made heaven, and earth, and the sea, and the fountains of waters.*"

John goes on, brethren, to describe the destruction of the wicked under the message of the third angel, which follows, and finally he paints a brief picture of the saved: "Here is the patience of the saints: here are they *that keep the commandments of God,* and the faith of Jesus" [verse 12].

I cannot dispense with my Creator-God, Beloved. When He returns I must be among those who have kept the commandments, including the Sabbath one. You see, Joe Wescott needs *re-creating,* if I am to be a fit member of the family of God, and every Sabbath when I worship Him, I am assured that He who was able to think a planet into existence and furbish it with beauty is well able to take the sinner, Joe Wescott, and make him pure too.

I can no longer stand in this pulpit on Sunday mornings believing as I do. I rest my case with you. May the God who loves us all richly bless you.

(There is no conversation as the congregation leaves the church. It is a stunned and quiet people who shake hands with their beloved young pastor. Finally only Joe, Michael, Sunlight, Jean, and her children remain.)

Jean *(close to tears):*   I can't believe you really went through with it, Joe. Everything you have worked so hard to build here for five years, gone in less than an hour. You have betrayed these people.

Joe: No, Jean, I would have betrayed them to keep on preaching error when I knew the truth. Michael you already know. Let me introduce you to Meg. We all played sandlot baseball together somewhere in the long ago. Meg, my wife, Jean. My daughter, Tammie, and my son, Jason.

(Meg extends her hand warmly to Joe's fragile blond wife, his curly-topped daughter, and his sober twelve-year-old son.)

Jason: What are you going to do now, Dad? You know, they aren't going to open these doors on Saturday, however right you are.

Joe: I have already accepted a position as a counselor in the city's department of social services. Thanks to Michael here, we shall not go hungry for the moment, anyhow. You said, "However right you may be." Does that mean you are with me, Son?

Jason: It makes sense to me. I know a girl at school who goes to church on Saturday. Once the teacher asked her to explain to the class why she couldn't go on Saturday outings, and she made it perfectly clear. I've half believed it ever since.

(Joe takes his family home, and Sunlight and Michael drive to an inn on the outskirts of the city for dinner.)

Michael: Was Carol reluctant to stay with Sybil after her long absence?

Sunlight: Not at all. Bill adores her—and spoils her. Carol couldn't wait to get down to their apartment. I am concerned about Sybil. She has changed somehow.

Michael: Less friendly?

Sunlight: No, she's her same dear self, and as beautiful as ever, but I had the feeling she was uncomfortable when I was telling her the things we've been studying while she's been sunning on the Mediterranean. The weeks with Bill, I fear, have been so rewarding to her after all the lonely years that she feels need of little else. She said she had neglected her Bible badly, and that our studies together seemed like something out of the far past. She and Bill are like young lovers. It's nice to see, yet frightening. Like there's no room in her life for God anymore. No room for anyone except Bill. When I mentioned that you and I were worshiping in our own way by ourselves on Saturdays, Bill laughed and said, "Meg, aren't you and Michael off that kick yet?" I don't think Sybil could take that kind of ridicule from him—she loves him so much. And she would be so afraid of losing him.

Michael: Well, we'll have to talk to her alone sometime. If it were not for her, you and I would still have nothing more on our minds than where to go out on Saturday night. We owe her a great deal.

(They sit in comfortable silence for a long time.)

Michael: I want to ask you something, Maggie. And I want your full attention.

Sunlight: You sound almost as serious as Joe did in the pulpit.

Michael: I'm at least as scared as he was.

Sunlight: You don't have to be afraid to ask me anything, Michael. You have been so kind to me that I would do anything on earth to make you happy.

Michael: Like marrying me?

Sunlight *(startled):*   You mustn't joke, Michael, on a day when Joe has been through such an ordeal.

Michael *(taking her hands in his):*   I'm not joking, Maggie. I love you. Maybe I always have, but these last months as we've searched to really know Jesus Christ and His plan for us, I've seen the strength and kindness of you developing and the hurt and bitterness receding. When you were hurt and grieving, I hurt for you. Now when you are healed and growing, I treasure every moment with you. Whatever lies ahead, and Joe doesn't think it's going to be easy, I'd like us to be in it together. You don't have to answer me now, Love. Take your time and think about it.

Sunlight *(her eyes full of tears):* Michael, I don't have to think about it. I have never entertained the thought of marrying you, though I've often felt guilty for consuming so much of your time when you should have been out meeting others. For so long I was far too hurt to even think of marriage, and I knew how you felt about the insecurity of life, so I thought we were the perfect friends. But just now as you were speaking, I suddenly saw you, *really saw you.* And I realized I'd never loved anyone so much in all my life. Not even Jim. Jim and I shared good times and children and our youth, but you and I have found Christ together, and that has added a beautiful dimension to our relationship. *I love you, Michael. (She laughs in wonder at her discovery, her face radiant with joy.)* I really do!

Michael: Today Joe lost everything, and I've gained everything. Oh, Maggie, let's order two salads and get out of here. We'll go home and tell Carol.

(It is the following Sabbath. Joe; Michael; Sunlight; Carol; Joe's son, Jason; and Sybil are gathered in Sunlight's living room.)

Michael: Carol has something to tell you before we go on to other matters. I don't think she can hold it much longer.

Carol: Are you all listening? I must have absolute quiet. *(She pauses.)* My mom and Michael are going to get married.

(There is a moment of silence, then a babble of congratulations.)

Sunlight: Michael's parents have given us their old summer home on a lake in the Adirondacks as a wedding present. We have planned our wedding for Sunday, June 10. We just want a very simple, out-of-doors ceremony, with Joe tying the knot. What would you all think of spending the weekend in the mountains, and maybe we could have a baptism the Sabbath before the wedding? Perhaps Bill would enjoy coming with us, Sybil, and maybe you could talk Jean and Tammie into coming, too, Joe. Both our parents are far away, and we have discouraged them from making the long trip, so you could be our family.

Sybil: It all sounds like a little bit of heaven, but I don't know whether Bill would consent to go or not, and you do understand I couldn't leave him, don't you?

Sunlight: Of course, but try to talk him into it.

Joe: I think it would be good for Jean and the children to get away for a weekend. I hope she will agree.

Michael: Joe, now *you* must tell us how your church accepted your sermon. Surely you have heard from them by now.

Joe: Indeed I have. The congregation sent five of the elders to talk with me. Five good men with whom I have worked and prayed, and in whom I have every confidence. They were deeply moved as they told me sadly that the church had voted to release me from my pastorate. I assured them that I realized there was little else they could do and that I would always hold each member in my heart and prayers in a very special way.

However, some interesting things have happened since. Two couples in the church came to my door one evening and asked to talk a bit. They were deeply impressed with the material I had presented and told me if I was starting a new church that would worship on Saturday, they were prepared to join me. I told them we had no organized group, but several of us had been studying together, and we planned to keep it informal for the time being. They have asked to meet with us. I hope it meets with your approval. Roy and Ellen are in their early thirties, bright, well-educated young people. Dale and Anne run a small printing business in Churchville. They're independent thinkers, not the type to follow the crowd down any road.

Sunlight: Why, Joe, that's worth all you went through. Of course, they may meet with us. There's a girl at work who's studying, and I think she'll soon be wanting fellowship too. I just share with her the things we've been discovering, and she's excited about it all. Goes home at night and checks out everything I've told her in the Bible.

Joe: And there's more. An elderly man called me just last night. Mr. Laird, a long-time member of my church. He told me he had studied the question of the Sabbath out for himself long ago after reading a book called *The Great Controversy*. He, too, assured me he was ready to take a stand on the Sabbath.

Jason: And don't forget me. You know I'm with you, Dad.

Joe *(fondly):* That's what's kept me going, Son.

Sunlight: Joe, I still haven't licked this smoking business. I'm down to one or two cigarettes a day but can't get over that last hump. I will not be baptized until that stinking habit is out of my life. That gives me two months. What do you suggest?

Joe: I have the feeling, Meg, you're trying to wrestle this out yourself. You've reached a certain point beyond which you can't go. God is showing you that without Him you can do nothing. We each have to learn that. Turn this problem over to the Lord and forget it. In fact, turn over to Him your entire life. Let Him do with you as He will. But there is something you *can* do—no, *must* do. Spend every spare moment with Him. Search out the promises of the Bible and use them as your armor against the devil. You will find that the closer you come to Him, the less you are attracted to the ugly things of this world.

Michael: I went through the same hassle with beer, Meg. In the end, I fasted and prayed for several days, just turning my entire life over to God's will as Joe suggested. I think sometimes God has to let us flounder around a long time before we understand that we are helpless to win the war ourselves. I found it a great relief when I finally gave up the struggle and let Him do battle for me. It means accepting His timing, which, of course, is not always ours. It isn't easy to yield up control of one's life, but I had grown so tired of my own failure that His outstretched hand was mighty welcome.

Sybil: I would like you all to pray for me. When I am with you I realize how I've slipped away from God during these months Bill and I have been in Europe. I do not have the same enthusiasm I once felt.

Michael: Just start digging into the Bible again, Sybil, and it will all come back. Meg and I have been concerned about you, and we refuse to let you lose everything you had gained, for all that means so much to us today we owe to you. Even our marriage, for if Meg had not found Christ, I do not think she would ever have been capable of loving again.

Sybil *(obviously moved):* I shall try, Michael, but having Bill all to myself has so filled my life with joy that I have felt little need of anything else. Bill says religion was just like my needlepoint and volunteer work at the hospital—something to stave off loneliness. He thinks it's a crutch and that we should stand on our own two feet and face up to problems in our own strength.

Joe: He's not alone in that thinking. It's quite popular today. Self-reliance is the password in America. It does have its place, but I fear our mental institutions are filled with men and women who needed God but who had been taught to handle life on their own. *Only* when we have Christ are we able to stand to our full stature and develop all our talents. Without Him, we will always be stunted and crippled. In that sense He *is* a crutch.

But now I must go home. Let's plan on the weekend of the tenth of June for a wedding and a baptism. Is it OK if my little group from the church comes along? Perhaps your friend at the store might like to join us, Meg?

(They chat a few more moments, then go to their separate homes. Michael, Sunlight, and Carol pack a lunch, take their Bibles, and set off for the country to spend the remainder of the Sabbath.)

(Two months later at the summer home in the Adirondacks, a small group has gathered at the shore in readiness for the baptism about to take place.)

Sunlight: This place is so beautiful, Michael. How can we ever thank your parents? How come you weren't more excited about the gift?

Michael: I have memories of being very lonely here, and bored. I guess as an only child I was lonely and bored almost anywhere away from my playmates in the city. It sort of took my breath away yesterday, when we drove in, to think all this was really ours. But the house needs a lot of work done on it. Dad warned me of that.

Sunlight: We can come up on our vacation and get at it. It would be fun. Have you noticed since you stopped smoking how good everything tastes and smells? I still can't believe that God has set me free, and it sure was God. I was licked!

Michael: It's a whole new life, Maggie. I feel so great, I have to pinch myself every morning to be sure I'm still on this wretched old planet.

Joe: Let's sing some hymns.

(For a time their singing fills the small cove and prompts an occasional canoeist to stop paddling. When the sun burns through the mists, warming the waters a bit, Joe asks each candidate for baptism to share a portion of Scripture especially meaningful to him before he goes down into the water.

He then baptizes the two young couples and the elderly man from his own church. Meg's friend does not feel she is yet ready. Finally, Michael and Sunlight move down into the chilly, sun-dappled water.)

Joe: Do you, Michael and Meg, have anything you want to share before you take this step?

Michael *(hesitantly, at first):* Until I found Jesus Christ, there was a great gap in my life. I felt that humanity was the victim of some irresponsible tyrant who had created a world and then gone off and left it topsy-turvy. Only when I understood what God was willing to do through His Son to recoup Adam's loss was I able to function as a whole person. A realization of what happened at the cross filled me with such blinding joy that I will never lose the wonder of it. I gladly pledge to follow Christ wherever He may choose to lead me.

Sunlight: Christ has enabled me to survive a divorce and the loss of a child and has given me the wonder of Michael's love. But even more than that, He has given me the assurance of *His* love, which would sustain me if everything else was stripped away. I can hardly grasp that His death was for *me* and *my* sins. Joe has told me that

Christ would have gone through it all for me alone, had no others responded. All eternity will not be long enough for me to absorb that.

(Joe places first Michael, then Sunlight, beneath the water, and they walk hand in hand toward the shore, where their friends wrap them in blankets. They all spend the rest of the day walking together in the surrounding countryside, stopping now and then to read together from their Bibles or just to rejoice over the new and wonderful peace they are experiencing. Sometimes they sing, and finally at sunset they gather on a cliff to pray.

Strong ties of fellowship knit them together. Only Sybil's absence mars the day. Mr. Laird, the elderly man, seems not to feel out of place with the younger folk. They all sense something very precious is taking place.)

(The next day Sunlight and Michael take their vows in a meadow of wild flowers bounded by the bouldered shore. Sunlight wears an oatmeal-colored peasant dress, and Carol has made her a bouquet of old-fashioned pink roses from a bush at the back door. Roy plays his guitar while the group sings What God Has Joined Together. *Joe performs a simple ceremony, and in moments, two who have been friends so long become man and wife.*

Later, when they have eaten the wedding luncheon on the terrace overlooking the lake, they chat for a bit before the guests leave for their homes.)

Joe: This weekend has been a bit of paradise. We have grown closer, and I have a feeling these friendships will endure through eternity. But I must talk to you all before we go back to the practical realities of life. As I study, and of late I have not put my Bible aside until the wee hours of the morning many a night, I can only conclude that some very somber events lie ahead of us. Already we see even more trouble brewing in far places, much unrest and scandal in our government here at home, and the nation's economy in a very perilous state. As I study the prophecies, I foresee that there will be a troubled time for those who obey the commandments of God. In fact, I think the time may come when we will be wise to remove ourselves from the city and live simply off the land.

Jean: Joe, you sound like a prophet of doom. This is a land of religious freedom. You told me yourself that groups have worshiped on Saturday for years.

Joe: That is true, but there have been many calamities on earth lately [Mark 13:7, 8], and people are uneasy. There is a strong feeling that if man would go back to the kind of reverence this country once knew, maybe God would smile upon us again. The first step is to urge, if not enforce, an old-fashioned observance of Sunday as a religious day, rather than the day of recreation it has become. I think you can see what that might do to religious freedom for those who do not consider Sunday the Sabbath. Already there is strong push in this direction . . . The state harassed by the church. Always when organized religion begins to pressure government there is trouble. It was such trouble that brought the original settlers to these shores.

(He smiles now.) But, I didn't mean to bring a worrisome element into our day of good things. We have chosen a little-used path, but Christ said, "Strait is the gate, and narrow is the way, which leadeth unto life, and *few there be that find it*" [Matthew 7:14], so that's encouraging for us.

Sunlight: Strangely enough I read that verse just the other day, and the one that precedes it, which says, "Wide is the gate, and broad is the way, that leadeth to destruction, and *many there be* which go in thereat.'' It made me realize truth has never been popular with the multitudes.

Jean: Does it really say that, Meg? Why didn't you ever point that out to me, Joe? I always felt you couldn't be right, when all the world kept Sunday, even though your presentation of the seventh-day Sabbath seems clear enough.

Joe *(hugging her):* Well, I never knew which text it was your heart needed to hear, but I'm glad it surfaced for you.

Now, let's all get out of here and let Michael and Meg have the place to themselves. Their week of honeymoon will fly by all too quickly. C'mon, Carol. Sybil will be expecting you. In fact a little bird told me she and Bill have quite a week planned for you.

(That evening Michael and Sunlight sit on the boulders bordering the lake, dabbling their feet in the moonlit waters gently lapping the shore. Only the sound of night creatures and a sighing in the pines breaks the stillness.)

Michael: Do you realize, Maggie, there's no one within twenty miles of us? Dad loved the isolation here and never complained about that cow path one has to drive along to get here. I didn't much appreciate it when I was younger, but now I understand why he loved it. It has made me feel very close to him this weekend.

Sunlight: It was a beautiful gift that will bring us hours and hours of pleasure. Tomorrow I shall write them how much we love it here. It's still like a dream that we are married. Loving you is so much better than liking you. I can't believe we'll be together always, even for eternity. It's just too good to be true.

Michael: I love you, Maggie Murphy. For the first time in years I am totally happy. God has answered the questions that were burning me out inside, and then He gave me you to heal the loneliness I'd known all my life.

Sunlight: What do you think about Joe's parting speech? Do you think he's overly concerned?

Michael: I don't want to frighten you, but I'm in full agreement with him. I spent some of those wee-hour sessions with him. He does not feel the books of Daniel and Revelation are closed books at all. In fact, at the end of Revelation it says, "Seal not the sayings of the prophecy of this book" [Revelation 22:10]. Daniel was told when he completed his writings: "Go thy way, Daniel: for the words are closed up and sealed *till the time of the end*" [Daniel 12:9]. So Joe has been searching for whatever light the two books shed upon our day. He has concluded there is but little time left, and what there is will be a challenge to God's people. He knows from his study of Hebrews that Christ is acting as our intercessory High Priest in heaven now, but he feels that the earth has about used up God's mercy and that Michael, which is another name for Christ [compare Jude 9; 1 Thessalonians 4:16; John 5:28], will soon stand up, as Daniel predicted in chapter 12, verse 1. When that happens there will be a time of trouble such as never was.

Sunlight: That *is* frightening. People are just going about their everyday activities with no idea that all of this is to take place. What will become of us?

Michael: There's a very comfortable statement in that same verse, Darling: "And at that time thy people shall be delivered." Thank God, we learned in time to turn to Christ for salvation.

Sunlight: What are we going to do about Sybil? Her great fear is that Bill will go back to his old life-style, and she will be without him again, so she simply doesn't cross him in any way, not even to come to our wedding. I always thought we'd be baptized together. But now I have a terrible fear that she will just slip away from God. I don't foresee losing her friendship, for she and Bill are both too attached to Carol, but it won't be the same if we can't share all we learn with her.

Michael: We must do our best to keep her in contact with Christ—she came close to a full surrender.

You know, Meg, I've been thinking that the time may come that this place will be a refuge for those of us who were here this weekend. If persecution lies ahead for those who believe the seventh-day Sabbath is significant, we would be safest out of the mainstream of civilization. This summer maybe you and I and Joe and Jean could spend our weekends and vacation here getting the place into a more livable condition.

Sunlight: Sybil told me that even Bill feels hard times are ahead. He's afraid, with the economy in such a shaky condition, that there will be looting and rioting in the cities before long. He once felt that he had plenty of money to live well for the rest of his days but now says that inflation has reduced his savings and investments alarmingly.

Michael: I think everywhere people are aware that time is running out. You know that widespread famine has brought death to millions in the lesser-developed countries. The earthquakes and tornadoes and airplane disasters [Mark 13:7, 8] don't even make the front page anymore. It's almost as though God has been withdrawing His protecting care, and Lucifer is having free reign at last.

Sunlight: Let's fix this place up so that we could even stay here in the winter if necessary. And we'll plant a huge garden, and I'll can a lot.

Michael: Which reminds me, I want you to give notice at work that you're through. Without a family, I've been able to put a good amount aside over the years, and I want you home with Carol.

Sunlight *(her eyes wide with joy):* You really mean it? You're so good to me. I can survive whatever lies ahead if you're with me. *(She shivers.)* This mountain air is getting to me. Let's go in.

Who could have dreamed that October day when Sunlight blew around the corner of Ridge and Genesee that her world would change so completely in less than a year? That intense young man, Joe, is quite right, though he will find few to listen. Quicker than he thinks, trouble will come upon those who honor all ten of the commandments. But I would say to them all, not just Sunlight and Michael and their friends, but those others around the earth who answer the call to come out of her, that there is a special promise for them in the last book of the Bible: "Blessed are they *that do his commandments,* that they may have right to the tree of life, and may enter in through the gates into the city" [Revelation 22:14].

I shall have a very special welcome on that day for Sunlight and her friends. The world little understands, because it has not immersed itself in God's Word, that the matter of the Sabbath is a test to God's people, just as the tree in the Garden of Eden was a test to Adam and Eve. It may seem a small matter, but it involves the great issue of loyalty to God.

I shall always be grateful that Earth Friend didn't pass by Sunlight and Michael, though they appeared most unlikely candidates for this land.

Chapter Ten

Two years have passed. The Prince has left the temple [Daniel 12:1] with the solemn decree: "He that is unjust, let him be unjust still: and he which is filthy, let him be filthy still: and he that is righteous, let him be righteous still: and he that is holy, let him be holy still. And, behold, I come quickly; and my reward is with me, to give every man according as his work shall be" [Revelation 22:11, 12].

Mankind now has no second chance. Long the Rebel has assured men that they need not fear, that even if they missed the rapture (another theory he prepared to lull them to sleep), that there'd be another chance later on. That tactic worked so well in Eden—"Ye shall not surely die"—that he's been using variations of it ever since. Those who believed him, without searching the Bible for themselves, no longer have an opportunity to receive the Prince's gift of salvation. Sadness fills heaven, for there are those we loved who simply could not tear themselves away from their activities long enough to hear the pleading voice of Earth Friend.

But, on the other hand, a quiet undertone of hope and anticipation pervades heaven, for we also heard Him say, "Behold, I come quickly," and we know the reunion cannot be far off. However, there is nothing on earth at the moment to indicate that any joyful event lies upon the horizon. The first angel has poured out his vial of sores upon the earth, and humanity suffers greatly [Revelation 16:2]. My eyes are riveted upon the little group in the mountains of New York State, and I am concerned for their safety. They are only a few among countless hundreds of thousands who have held fast

125

their allegiance to the Word of God. May it all be over soon.

(Sunlight, Michael, and Carol, with Joe, Jean, Tammie, and Jason, are at the home in the Adirondacks. With them, too, are Roy and Ellen, Dale and Anne. Also Mr. Laird and Sunlight's young friend, Kelly, whom she met in the store. Sorrow and tragedy ravage the earth. Dale, bearing several newspapers, has just returned from a trip into town to purchase rubber rings for canning, a few expensive, precious gallons of gas for the generator, and some staples. The rest are gathered about the table eating their evening meal.)

Dale: Hope you saved something for me. I'm famished. Had a strange conversation with the storekeeper today. He asked me if we were one of those crazy communes he'd read about. Said he thought they died out in the seventies. When I said we weren't, then he asked me why we *were* up here anyway. I told him we thought the cities were no longer safe or healthful and that we hoped to survive simply off the land. Guess that satisfied him that we were harmless, if a bit crazy.

Then after I got into the jeep and read a few headlines, I was glad that I had not brought religion into the discussion. Look. *(He holds up a newspaper with the bold headline "SUNDAY OBSERVANCE ENFORCED. VIOLATORS WILL BE PROSECUTED." Joe and Michael exchange glances, but they drop the discussion until the children are in bed and the adults have gathered about a blazing fire in the beamed living room. However, it is October, and a chill soon creeps into the room. Joe, as the acknowledged leader of the group, reads to them from the newspapers.)*

Joe: Here's an article about a new health problem in the South Pacific. It seems the population of entire cities are afflicted with excruciatingly painful sores that antibiotics won't touch. My friends, we are closer than we dreamed. *(He turns to his son.)* Would you read Revelation 16:2, please?

Jason: "And the first [angel] went, and poured out his vial upon the earth; and there fell a noisome and grievous sore upon the men which had the mark of the beast, and upon them which worshipped his image."

Joe: It's my guess that the first of the seven plagues is being poured out. The sores, coupled with the decree that those refusing to worship on Sunday will be prosecuted, are warning flags to the Bible student.*

Sunlight *(worry shadowing her face):* But what's the mark of the beast and his image? Will the plagues fall on us?

Joe: I'll answer your last question first, or better yet, let's let God answer it. Open your Bibles to Psalm 91. Let's read the first twelve verses:

"He that dwelleth in the secret place of the most High shall abide under the shadow of the Almighty. I will say of the Lord, He is my refuge and my fortress: my God; in him will I trust. Surely he shall deliver thee from the snare of the fowler, and from the noisome pestilence. He shall cover thee with his feathers, and under his wings shall thou trust: his truth shall be thy shield and buckler. Thou shalt not be afraid for the terror by night; nor for the arrow that flieth by day; nor for the pestilence that walketh in darkness; nor for

---

*It is the author's intention here, and in later chapters, only to give a general idea of how the plagues, outlined in Revelation 16, *may* take place. It would not seem that these plagues could be universal, lest the early ones eliminate the earth's population before the later ones should fall. Let the reader be alerted that the author has taken the liberty, for the sake of the story, of naming definite geographical locations and time concepts relating to the plagues for which there is no Biblical basis. God Himself will determine where and when the plagues will fall, and over how long a period.

the destruction that wasteth at noonday. A thousand shall fall at thy side, and ten thousand at thy right hand; but it shall not come nigh thee. Only with thine eyes shalt thou behold and see the reward of the wicked. Because thou hast made the Lord, which is my refuge, even the most High, thy habitation; there shall no evil befall thee, neither shall any plague come nigh thy dwelling. For he shall give his angels charge over thee, to keep thee in all thy ways. They shall bear thee up in their hands, lest thou dash thy foot against a stone.''

Kelly: That's absolutely beautiful. I think we should learn it and say it every night together through whatever lies ahead for us.

Joe: Good idea, Kelly. Before we leave this matter, let me read you Revelation 18:4: "And I heard another voice from heaven, saying, Come out of her, my people, that ye be not partakers of her sins, and *that ye receive not of her plagues.''*

Now, Meg, as to the mark of the beast. The prophecies of Daniel and Revelation are complex, and I do not pretend to understand them in their fine details. I do think, however, that I can safely say that the beasts in both Daniel and Revelation represent the various phases of Satan's evil work through the ages . . . his attempts to stamp out truth and the followers of Jesus. In contrast, Scripture usually represents Christ by a lamb [Revelation 13:8; Revelation 14:1; Isaiah 53:7; John 1:29; Revelation 5:6]. I think the symbolism is obvious here. It seems that just before Christ returns, some power, labeled here as the "image of the beast," arises to carry out the same cruel purposes as the beast had in earlier times. It is the followers of this beast and its image upon which the plagues will fall.

Jean: Please be more specific, Joe. What do you think the beast and its image represent today?

Joe: I believe it to be any power that would deny man his freedom to worship God as he sees fit. To be even more specific, those powers today that are forcing men to worship upon a day which God has never set aside as holy. Daniel describes a power that shall "think to change times and laws" [Daniel 7:25], which is exactly what happened when the true Sabbath was subtly eased offstage centuries ago, and we will see an attempt to do the same again in our time. This power attempting to wrench from God His authority has been active in every age, under different guises, and all spring from Lucifer's hatred for Christ.

Jean: But don't those who think differently than you have a right to disagree?

Joe: By all means, but not to *force* their convictions upon others. Force, which always leads to persecution, has no part in the kingdom of Jesus Christ. He must weep for the blood shed in His name.

Mr. Laird: How serious do you think the situation will be?

Joe: Let's all turn to Revelation 13:15. *(He reads the verse aloud.)*

"And he [the beast] had power to give life unto the image of the beast, that the image of the beast should both speak, and cause that as many as would not worship the image of the beast should be killed."

That's how serious it will become, Fred, before we're finished. But don't forget the psalm we just read. God will see us through.

Michael: I want to share with you a text I found today that really had meaning for me and should for all of us. *(He turns to Revelation 12:17.)* Before I read, let me explain that the dragon always represents Satan, and the woman stands for the church. Now listen to this:

"And the dragon [Satan] was wroth with the woman [the church], and went to make war with the *remnant of her seed, which keep the commandments of God,* and have the testimony of Jesus."

Now it seems to me we must be the remnant, not just us, but all those who are attempting to be true commandment-keepers today when it is becoming so difficult. In view of this verse, I don't think we should be surprised that Satan is stirring up trouble for those who honor the seventh-day Sabbath.

Jean: Sometimes I think we have made the Sabbath our whole religion.

Ellen: I think the Sabbath *is* a vital factor at this moment in time, because it was something very special and important that God gave us. Then for generations it was lost, at least to the majority of people. Now it is found and has become an issue. It is a sign of our obedience or lack of it, just as the tree of knowledge of good and evil was in the Garden of Eden.

But I think that all of us here know that the focal point of everything we believe is the cross. Without what happened there that day on Calvary, it wouldn't make any difference whether we kept Saturday or Wednesday. Nothing would matter at all, for we would die and rot in our graves. I personally honor the Sabbath because it's one way I can show Christ I appreciate what He did for me and because I feel especially close to Him on that day. It's my special visiting day with Him.

I have never forgotten what Joe said in his last sermon at the church about his Creator-God. When I observe the seventh day in honor of Creation, I'm assured that God will *re-create* me in His image.

(Suddenly flustered, Ellen laughs.) Well, that was quite a speech for me, but I wanted to share with you, Jean, how I feel the cross and the Sabbath are all tied together.

(Jean makes no reply and shortly leaves the group

for her room.)

Sunlight: I noticed in Revelation 15 a beautiful description of those who didn't succumb to the power of the beast and his image. Let me read it to you:

"And I saw as it were a sea of glass mingled with fire: and them that had gotten the victory over the beast, and over his image, and over his mark, and over the number of his name, stand on the sea of glass, having the harps of God. And they sing the song of Moses the servant of God, and the song of the Lamb, saying, Great and marvellous are thy works, Lord God Almighty; just and true are thy ways, thou King of saints" [verses 2 and 3].

God's people will triumph. That makes everything worthwhile. Even living crowded here and winter coming on with little to eat or money to buy more.

Roy: Or heat. I think it's time to crawl into our bunks. I can feel the frost coming in through all the cracks.

(They disperse for the night, and the fire burns down to a few sparks among the ashes.)

In the following months they go to the store less often, preferring to keep to themselves as much as possible, but the occasional paper they do acquire confirms Joe's predictions. The ocean becomes afflicted with a mysterious "algae" that leaves the waves clotted with a stagnant red mass resembling blood. The marine life dies and washes, stinking and rotten, onto the shores [Revelation 16:3]. An evening in late March finds the group huddled about the fireplace once more, this time wrapped in blankets and obviously suffering with the cold. A candle flickers on the table as Michael reads from the Book of Isaiah. The men crack black walnuts, and the women pick the meats from the shells. The sound of a snowmobile breaks the stillness outside.

Kelly: What is a snowmobile doing out here at this hour?

(Tension fills the room, each member of the group

well aware that beyond their quiet retreat there have been difficulties for the followers of God.)

Michael: Perhaps someone is lost, and we can be of help. *(The sound draws closer, then the engine is cut, and a knock sounds upon the door. Michael answers it, finding Jim upon the doorstep.)* Jim, what on earth brings you here in such weather? Come in. Not that we have much heat to offer you, but it's definitely an improvement over the outside.

(Several move away from the fire to make a spot closer to the heat for him.)

Sunlight: Why have you come, Jim? It had to be something important to bring you on such a journey. Carol will be wild with joy when she finds you here in the morning.

Jim: I won't be here in the morning, Meg. I have come to take Carol back with me. You must all listen to me carefully and take me seriously. I came here at night, for it is not healthy to mingle with, or aid, those observing the seventh-day Sabbath. It is not safe for Carol to be here, Meg. Marie and I will keep her until this all blows over, as surely it will.

The rest of you, if you insist upon making an issue of this Sabbath business, had best lay low. Those who agree with you, but are not so fortunately hidden away, have faced some most unpleasant situations. They're finding it increasingly difficult to buy or sell anything [Revelation 13:16, 17], which is, of course, making ordinary living almost impossible. They are constantly on television and in the papers as they go on trial for their beliefs. Surprisingly, their numbers are not declining but rapidly increasing. It seems there are thousands who have had some sleeping convictions upon this matter and who are now willing to take a stand upon it, which I find odd. *(He shrugs.)* But, then, human nature always has been unpredictable.

To make matters worse, as you know, some mysterious problem has afflicted the water supply of the entire eastern half of the country. At first it was just the ocean, but now there's no pure water to be had, and we're dependent on what's shipped to us. You can't believe the mayhem it has caused. By the way, what have you been doing? melting snow?

Joe: We weren't aware of the problem. Our drinking water's fine—comes from a deep well.

Jim: You can't give the well the credit. Wells haven't been any cleaner than streams. Everything is choked with that miserable, revolting red mass [Revelation 16:4].

You see, the world is in a mess, what with those wretched sores they're experiencing in the islands and the water problems here. Everyone's a little edgy and looking for someone to pin the blame on, which makes those of you who insist on breaking with religious tradition likely victims.

Michael: But what are your personal convictions, Jim?

Jim: I'll admit I've done quite a bit of studying ever since Meg explained to me why you were moving up here, and I can't argue with your theology. There simply isn't much basis for keeping Sunday that I can find, but I have no intention of putting my neck on the chopping block just because of that. My conclusion is that things are going to get worse before they get better.

Joe: They're never going to get better, Jim—at least in the way you think. When these calamities are over, Christ will return. Study the Book of Revelation carefully and take a courageous stand, my friend. It will not be long until we see our Lord's deliverance of mankind. It's not a time to dally with indecision.

Jim *(turning to Meg):* Why don't you awaken Carol and get her things packed? Dress her warmly. It's a bitter journey down to the road. Michael, do you have anything you can haul supplies on? I brought some staples for you, thinking it may have been quite a while since you've been able to get out.

Sunlight: Thank you for your kindness, Jim. Whatever you have brought us will be a godsend, for we've been living very carefully on our limited supplies. To be quite honest we're amazed our food has stretched as long as it has.

But about Carol. Much as I appreciate what you and Marie are willing to do, I really don't want her to go. She understands the issues involved and is content here in spite of the hardships.

Jim: Will you let *her* make that decision, Meg? Will you get her up and ask her? It's cold here. She must be terribly uncomfortable all the time.

Michael: There's a trusty old wood stove in the sleeping area, Jim. She's not had a sniffle all winter in spite of the drafts around here. Her diet has been adequate. But we *will* get her up, for she would be heartbroken if you left without seeing her. *(He leaves and returns with Carol, who runs into her father's arms joyfully.)*

Jim: Hi, Baby. I've come to take you home until your mother and Michael decide to come back to the city. I've worried about you here.

Carol *(eyes troubled):* I love you, Daddy, but I can't go home with you. Michael and Mom and Joe and Jean and all the rest of us believe that Jesus is coming soon. The Bible says there will be trouble for everyone just before He returns, and we're safer here than you and Marie are in the city. Uncle Bill himself said there would be violence in the cities sooner or later.

Sunlight: Speaking of Bill, how is Sybil doing?

Jim: When I decided to come, I stopped by her apartment to see if she had any message for you, and she sent you this letter. Good thing Carol reminded me. *(Meg tucks the letter in her jeans pocket for later reading.)* Carol, I think this decision is one your mother and I should make.

Carol: Do you want me to go, Mom? I would be so lonely for you all.

Sunlight: Jim, she is safe and well and content here.

Jim: She's not even getting an education. It's unnatural living like this.

Carol: No, Daddy, Ellen is a teacher, and she has school for Jason and Tammie and me every day. Pastor Joe and Michael teach us all kinds of interesting things, too, and we've learned so much about nature out here that I can tell you every kind of bird in these woods. I've learned more this winter than in two years of school. I listen while Michael teaches Jason algebra, and already I can do it, and I'm only in the fourth grade.

Sunlight *(laughing):* See, Jim, all is well with your little one.

Jim *(still concerned but obviously a bit relieved also):* Well, Button, if you're sure you want to stay here, I'm certainly not going to drag you away.

Carol *(climbing into his lap):* I want to be with you and Mom *both.* I wish you'd give your heart to Jesus and come up here with us. It feels so good to belong to Him. I could teach you easy, Daddy. Please.

(Jim sits troubled and quiet a moment. The group prays silently. Then he speaks, almost as though he has not heard the child upon his lap.)

Jim: I must be getting back, so if one of you fellows wants to ride down to the pickup with me, we'll pack the supplies onto the toboggan and haul them here. Then I'll be on my way.

Michael: We have a snowmobile here for emergency use, so we'll just ride down to the truck with you, and you won't have to come back. It's going to be a long drive to the city. You won't get much sleep tonight.

Joe: God bless you, Friend. It took courage to come, and I pray no harm will befall you because of it. We're more grateful for the food than you can know.

Jean: May I ask a favor of you, Jim?

Jim: Of course. What can I do for you?

Jean: I would like to ride back to the city with you. I've just packed my things.

Jim: Well, of course, if you're sure that's what you want.

Joe *(his face ashen):* Jean, you can't mean this. Let's go and talk it over privately before you make your decision.

Jean: There's nothing to say that I cannot say before the group. You may be right in your convictions, Joe, but I fear I'm not the type to defend noble causes. When I heard Jim say he wasn't putting his neck on the chopping block, even though this may be truth, I realized those were my senti- ments exactly. I want to get back into life. I hate being different. When we sold the house, I set aside some money for my personal use, fearing where your search would lead us. It's in a Rochester bank and will meet my needs until I can get a job. Tell the children that when I get settled and establish a home, I will come for them. Probably in May. I love you, Joe, but I cannot follow you down these strange paths. I'm sorry.

(She starts to leave the room, hesitates, and turns back.)

The rest of you need never fear to follow his leading. He's a good man. Take care of my kids, Meg, until I come. OK?

(Joe follows her out of the room. Michael and Roy get into their outer clothing to go with Jim, and in a few moments Jean returns with her suitcase. She and Joe cling together for a moment and then she leaves with

the men. Without a word, Joe goes to his room.)

Carol *(tears running down her face):* Tammie and Jason will be heartbroken in the morning. And their daddy.

Sunlight: We must do what we can to help all three of them bear this sorrow. Poor Jean. So many times I sensed it was not the same for her as for the rest of us. Her heart wasn't in it somehow.

Anne: Sometimes I get discouraged like that. I want to be back in civilization, just doing ordinary things again, but then I get out my Bible and read about the life of Jesus here on earth and I realize there must have been times when He wanted to be back in heaven doing ordinary things too. But for us, He stuck it out here on earth until His mission was fulfilled. Then I see our situation in a new perspective, an opportunity to suffer with Him. I don't think it can be too much longer.

(They chat quietly by the fire until Michael and Roy return with the toboggan load of supplies behind the snowmobile. Even after the men have piled the precious bags of oatmeal, flour, dried fruit, beans, and other things upon the table, no one feels like rejoicing, though the food is sorely needed and appreciated. Joe's sorrow rests heavily upon everyone.

When the rest have all drifted off to bed and Carol is once more sleeping, Michael and Meg still linger in the firelit room.)

Sunlight: How could Jean do it, just walk away from him without a word of warning?

Michael: I think he was more prepared than we know. Her dissatisfaction was often evident.

Sunlight: My heart aches for him. I've been there, and it hurts so bad. Maybe you should go in and talk to him.

Michael: I know Joe pretty well, Maggie. I think he will need to work this out by himself. You'll find in the morning he'll have pulled himself together. Don't forget, Joe has walked very closely with his God for a long time. He's not alone.

What did Sybil have to say?

Sunlight: Why, I've not even read the letter! In all this confusion I completely forgot it.

(She takes the envelope eagerly from her pocket and reads aloud.)

"Dear Meg,

"The world has turned upside down. The money Bill hoarded so carefully is of little value now in our deteriorating economy. He worries constantly. I fear for his health. I think of you all often and envy you your peace of mind. I put my love for Bill ahead of my love for God. I could not accept Michael's news of the Sabbath, for I did not want anything in my life that would be offensive to Bill. But my heart knew Michael was speaking truth. I am following in Revelation 16 the calamities taking place upon this earth and recognize them as the plagues outlined there. I long to be among those who meet Christ with rejoicing, but some deep inner sense tells me it is too late. I came so very close. Oh, Meg, what an emptiness descends upon me, when I think about it. I can write no more, for Jim is waiting. I doubt you will send Carol back with him, but be assured if you do that Bill and I will love and cherish her. Give her a hug for us. Michael too. I go now and then to Jen's grave. It comforts me somehow.

"Love,

"Sybil.

"PS   There are hundreds of thousands taking a firm

stand for the seventh day, now that it is an issue. Some others, who have observed it faithfully for years, now abandon their faith in the heat of persecution. Feeling runs strong against those who will not be swayed, and their lives are in danger daily. There is talk that they will be put to death. Sounds like the Inquisition. Bill hates them with a passion and says the quicker they are wiped out, the better. I hold my peace. Do not waver, my friend. SN"

Sunlight *(sobbing, flings herself into Michael's arms):*   Oh, Michael, I have had too much sorrow for one night. *Is it* too late for Sybil?

Michael: That is for God to decide, my darling. It has indeed been a sad day.

   (They kneel together, mingling tears with their prayers.)

And I have added my tears to theirs. Sybil's letter tore my heart out, for when the Prince left the temple and ceased His intercessory work, it was indeed too late. Not just for Sybil, but for millions of others. Early in the history of the earth, God said, "My spirit shall not always strive with man" [Genesis 6:3], and that sad hour has arrived. Earth Friend no longer works upon the hearts of humans, and the Rebel is free to exercise full control over them, with the exception of those written in the Lamb's book of life [Revelation 13:7, 8].

The plagues of heat and darkness and hail [Revelation 16] yet await mankind. Such destruction as men have never dreamed of will ravage that small planet, and the followers of the Prince scattered over its surface will live moment by moment through simple faith in His care. Sunlight and her friends are safely sealed [Revelation 7:1-4], but they have much hardship yet to endure. Their sufferings, however, are as nothing compared to those who are in more settled areas. Now that Earth Friend's influence is withdrawn, evil is free to flower, and the universe will tremble at the cruelty of man under the Rebel's control.

The Peaceful Kingdom is hushed these days, each citizen going about his work soberly. It is not a time for singing. The eyes of the Prince are often sad, yet now and then as He observes an earthling standing staunchly for Him under the most fearsome circumstances, His face is radiant with joy.

Chapter Eleven

The summer has passed in a flurry of activity for the little community in the Adirondacks. The believers have cut and stacked wood for the winter's fires, and an acre of garden has kept the group busy weeding, harvesting, and canning. The men have attempted to tighten the old house against another onslaught of frigid mountain weather. Their cash reserves are nearly depleted, but the men dare not go out into the surrounding communities to look for work, lest they bring upon themselves the persecution that rests so heavily upon others in the land.

(In the late afternoon Meg and Anne are shelling sunflower seeds on the front porch when a car drives cautiously along the narrow, overgrown path and into the front yard. Jean alights. Meg leaps down the steps and throws her arms around her.)

Sunlight: Jean, it's so good to see you. What brings you?

Jean: When the children chose to stay with you this spring I accepted it, knowing they were probably better off here in the mountains than cooped up in the city, especially with me working, but this time I have come to take them with me, and you can't change my mind.

Sunlight: Well, they'll surely welcome you. I know Tammie especially misses you. And it will do Joe a world of good to see you. He says little, but we know his heart is often heavy. Won't you come back to us? It's going to be a difficult winter, but the Lord will provide.

Jean: It's going to be a difficult winter everywhere, Meg. Something has gone all wrong on this planet. I know Joe feels these disasters are divinely predicted events, but I'm more inclined to agree with those who feel God is displeased with you who have broken away from traditional beliefs. Where is Joe?

Sunlight: All the men are in the woods sawing up fallen trees for the winter's fuel supply. Jason is helping them, and I think Tammie went along also. She makes herself useful in many ways. You will find the children thinner, but tanned and fit. If you just walk along the trail, you will soon locate them by sound, if not by sight.

(Jean sets off down the path, and Meg rounds up the women to plan a special supper in her honor.

Later the group gathers about the table, Tammie and Jason flanking their parents at the head. Joe looks happier than in many a day, and a festive mood prevails.)

Jean *(handing Carol a package and a letter):* I stopped by your dad's house to tell him I was coming, and he sent you this letter and a box of birthday presents. He also gave me money to purchase a lot of food for all. Said he thought I, having lived here with you, would know more about your needs than he would. It's out in the car.

Joe: Jim is a good man. He should be here with us. I hope no trouble ever comes upon him for his concern for us, or upon you either, Darling. *(He places his arm about Jean's shoulders.)* You really shouldn't have come. But now that you're here, I hope we can persuade you to stay.

Jean *(pulling away from her husband):* Joe, I told you frankly I came only to take the children back. It's no longer safe for them to be here with you. Sooner or later someone is going to discover this place and that you're here because of your religious convictions. There is a law about to pass calling for the lives of those who observe the seventh day [Revelation 13:15; Matthew 24:9]. Joe, the world is falling apart. You're hidden away here in the hills and losing touch with reality. The water supply in America is contaminated [Revelation 16:3, 4], Europe is staggering with famine under an intense heat that literally scorches men [Revelation 16:8], and the population in other areas is afflicted with sores beyond medical help [Revelation 16:2].* If we don't turn back to God, this planet will be wiped out. *Are you hearing me, Joe? (Her voice rises, and she pounds her fists upon the table in frustration.)* Get out of these mountains and take your place behind the pulpit where you belong.

Joe *(on the verge of tears):*   The truth can no longer be preached from a pulpit, Jean. I want you to think calmly about the very nature of persecution for a moment. Did Jesus Christ ever advocate killing, even for religious purposes? Did He destroy those who didn't agree with Him? I want to share with you something that John Wesley wrote long ago. *(He takes a small notebook from his pocket and reads.)*

"Condemn no man for not thinking as you think. Let every one enjoy the full and free liberty of thinking for himself. Let every man use his own judgment, since every man must give an account of himself to God. Abhor every approach, in any kind or degree, to the spirit of persecution. If you cannot reason or persuade a man into the truth, never attempt to force him into it. If love will not compel him to come, leave him to God, the Judge of all" ("Advice to the People Called Methodists," in his *Works* [Grand Rapids, Michigan, Zondervan—reprint of 1872 ed.], Vol. 8, p. 357).

Jean: But the persecution today is only to bring people back to a proper regard for God.

Michael: The persecution of the Dark Ages was sup-

---

*See footnote referring to plagues on page 127.

posedly for the same purpose. Jesus warned His followers that "the time cometh, that whosoever killeth you will think that he doeth God service" [John 16:2].

Jason: There's another verse, too, Mother. "All that will live godly in Christ Jesus shall suffer persecution." I think it is usually safer to be among the persecuted than the persecutors.

Jean: You won't think so, Jason, if they find you up here.

Jason: Not safer physically, perhaps, but spiritually. And this is a right cause, Mother. You know the first angel of Revelation 14 [verses 6, 7] calls for men to worship the God of *Creation.* How can you do that if you ignore the day He set aside in commemoration of Creation? The whole conflict between Christ and Lucifer had to do with the *creature's* willingness to accept his nature and role as a *created* being. It was Lucifer's thirst to be like God that got him into trouble. The Sabbath reminds us of our *need* of God as King and Ruler in our lives. If we reject the Sabbath, we only reflect Lucifer's distaste for bowing before our Maker as the Superior Being.

Jean *(smiling ironically):* Hear ye, hear ye! My son, the preacher.

Jason: This is no joke, Mother. The mark of the beast, which the third angel warns against in Revelation 14:9, is the worship of a false sabbath, for just a few verses later [Revelation 14:12] the saints are described as those who keep the commandments of God. You can't keep the commandments, Mom, if you reject the fourth one.

On what grounds can men take our lives if they have no Scripture to condemn us with?

Jean: The whole Christian community can't be wrong, Jason.

Jason: All through the ages, the protectors of truth have been in the minority. Remember the verse Dad taught us:

"Strait is the gate, and narrow is the way, which leadeth unto life, and few there be that find it" [Matthew 7:14]?

Jean *(rising impatiently):* If I am going to get back to the city before midnight, I must be on my way. You children get your things together, and someone should get the food out of the car.

Jason: I have never disobeyed you, Mother, but I wish to stay here with Dad.

Jean: You will have to trust me, Jason. I insist you go back with me.

(Jason looks questioningly at his father.)

Tammie: I don't want to go either, Mom. I wish you would stay here with us. I miss you so much.

Jean *(frustrated but determined):* You will both go, and no more discussion.

Joe: I believe the children are old enough to make their own decision, Jean. They know more about their Bibles than most adults.

Jean: How can you do this to me, Joe? Do you realize how frightened I am for them?

Joe: There is no safe place on the face of the earth, Jean. As yet we have suffered none of the disasters falling upon the planet. Our water runs clean and clear. We work hard and have little money, but there is simple food upon our table, and we have had no sickness. As for the death decree, you know the psalm we say together here nightly, my darling . . . "A thousand shall fall at thy side, and ten thousand at thy right hand; but it shall not come nigh thee" [Psalm 91:7].

If the children wish to go with you, I will not stand in their way, but if not, I beg you to let them remain here. And it is the fondest wish of my heart that you would stay yourself. *(His voice breaks.)*

Jean: I'm sorry I came. *(She, too, is close to tears.)* You have turned the children away from me. If it weren't for the trouble I'd bring upon them, I'd report you all to the police. Sybil Norris' husband would have done it long ago if it were not for his love for Carol. He hates everything you stand for, and so do I.

(She leaves without a backward glance, and the men follow her to bring Jim's gift of food to the house. Tammie turns, weeping, into her father's arms while Jason stands at the window with a deep hurt in his dark eyes.)

Joe *(taking his Bible):*   This is a hard hour for both of you, but the very ache in our hearts is a sign of the end. Mark says, "Now the brother shall betray the brother to death, and the father the son; and the children shall rise up against their parents, and shall cause them to be put to death. And ye shall be hated of all men for my name's sake: but he that shall endure unto the end, the same shall be saved" [Mark 13:12, 13].

In the loss of your mother *(his voice chokes)* I—I feel the weight of Christ's cross as I have never felt it before, but I ever remember that Adam brought our race to this point through his love for Eve. I cannot turn my back upon Jesus, even for your mother, whom I love more than anyone else upon the face of the earth. *(The children hug him, and their tears mingle.)*

(That evening Carol shares parts of her letter from her father with the group.)

"I saw Sybil on the street the other day. She told me Bill went to a popular faith healer here in the city and appears to have been cured of his heart problems, which had really been giving him trouble lately. There is a great deal of healing going on, all kinds of miracles and supernatural events [Matthew 24:24; Revelation 13:11-14].

One wonders what their source is [Revelation 16:14].

"Lately there has been much excitement over the various appearances of a being quite different than is normally seen on earth. He is a creature of rare beauty and purports to be Christ [Revelation 13:12-15; Mark 13:6; Matthew 24:23, 24]. Somehow he doesn't exactly fulfill my expectations of the Second Coming, but I must admit he is something out of the ordinary. It's been said he has called down fire from heaven in imitation, I suppose, of whomever it was who accomplished that feat in the Bible. Please share all this with your mom and Michael. They will probably have some rational explanation for it."

Tammie: Was it really Jesus, Daddy?

Joe: Turn in your Bible, Honey, to Matthew 24 and read verses 23 through 27.

Tammie: "Then if any man shall say unto you, Lo, here is Christ, or there; believe it not. For there shall arise false Christs, and false prophets, and shall shew great signs and wonders; insomuch that, if it were possible, they shall deceive the very elect. Behold, I have told you before. Wherefore if they shall say unto you, Behold, he is in the desert; go not forth: behold, he is in the secret chambers; believe it not. For as the lightning cometh out of the east, and shineth even unto the west; so shall also the coming of the Son of man be."

That means the sky will be full of His glory, and we will be full of His glory, and we'll be looking *up*, doesn't it, Daddy? Not watching Him on TV or seeing Him walking about the earth [Matthew 16:27; Matthew 24:30].

Joe: Absolutely. And He will announce nothing contrary to the teachings of the Bible.

Anne: What's going to happen after we get to heaven? I've never thought much beyond that point, I guess. In fact, what becomes of the wicked who are left behind on this earth when the resurrected and the living righteous are taken to heaven?

Joe: I guess in all our study of the events preceding the Second Coming, we've failed to put much emphasis on what follows it. It's perhaps the most exciting story of all.

Meg, will you read Revelation 20:6 for us, please?

Sunlight: "Blessed and holy is he that hath part in the first resurrection: on such the second death hath no power, but they shall be priests of God and of Christ, and shall reign with him a thousand years."

Joe: Now, Dale, how about sharing 1 Thessalonians 4:16, 17 with us?

Dale: "For the Lord himself shall descend from heaven with a shout, with the voice of the archangel, and with the trump of God: and the dead in Christ shall rise first: then we which are alive and remain shall be caught up together with them in the clouds, to meet the Lord in the air: and so shall we ever be with the Lord."

Carol: That's when Mom and I are going to see Jen again.

Joe: Right you are, Button. Is it clear to everyone from these verses that the righteous dead are raised and lifted up to meet Christ, followed by those righteous who are living on earth at the time of His coming?

Anne: Simple enough for a kindergartner. But what was that in the first text about a thousand years?

Joe: Let's go at this in an orderly manner. The righteous are in heaven with Christ, and Revelation 20:6 says they will reign with Christ a thousand years. Now let's see what we will be doing during that long period. I'm reading now from Revelation 20:4:

"And I saw thrones, and they sat upon them, and *judgment* was given unto them; . . . and they lived and reigned with Christ a thousand years."

OK. So for one thousand years we will be taking part in

a judgment of some kind going on in heaven. Judgment of whom? We find in 1 Corinthians 6:2 "that the saints shall judge the world." In fact, it continues, "Know ye not that we shall judge angels?" [verse 3; see also Jude 6]. Because Christ has already completed a work of judgment before His second coming, I suspect this later one will be an opening of heaven's records to satisfy the saved of God's justice. Evidently there will also be a judgment of those angels who fell with Lucifer.

Ellen: What happens to the living wicked at Christ's coming?

Joe: Luke 17:26-30 gives us the answer to that. Luke describes how the Flood came upon men as a surprise, even though they had been warned, and how fire and brimstone rained upon Sodom for its wickedness, and then he concludes, "Even thus shall it be in the day when the Son of man is revealed." [See also 2 Thessalonians 2:8.]

Michael: I read a description of that time in Revelation 6 the other day that made me feel they are probably destroyed simply by the glory of Christ. Only the pure can stand before that brightness. Let me read you the verses, starting with verse 14:

"And the heaven departed as a scroll when it is rolled together; and every mountain and island were moved out of their places. And the kings of the earth, and the great men, and the rich men, and the chief captains, and the mighty men, and every bondman, and every free man, hid themselves in the dens and in the rocks of the mountains; and said to the mountains and rocks, Fall on us, and hide us from the face of him that sitteth on the throne, and from the wrath of the Lamb: for the great day of his wrath is come; and who shall be able to stand?" *(He shakes his head.)* It will be an awesome day.

Joe: The fire's dying down. I don't know about the rest of you, but my eyes feel the strain of the poor light; so let's move on quickly so we can settle this question of the one thousand years. We know the saved who are in heaven are involved in some sort of judgment, and the wicked are destroyed by the brightness of His coming. Those wicked who were already in their graves sleep on. Revelation 20:5 says, "The rest of the dead lived not again until the thousand years were finished."

Jason: May I read the verses that tell where Satan is during that long period, Dad?

Joe: Sure thing.

Jason: "And I saw an angel come down from heaven, having the key of the bottomless pit and a great chain in his hand. And he laid hold on the dragon, that old serpent, which is the Devil, and Satan, and bound him a thousand years, and cast him into the bottomless pit, and shut him up, and set a seal upon him, that he should deceive the nations no more, till the thousand years should be fulfilled: and after that he must be loosed a little season" [Revelation 20:1-3].

Carol: What's the bottomless pit?

Joe: The bottomless pit is nothing more than the earth stripped of all life. The way Jeremiah describes such a situation it could pass for a bottomless pit all right. Here, let me find it. Listen:

"I beheld the earth, and, lo, it was without form, and void; and the heavens, and they had no light. I beheld the mountains, and, lo, they trembled, and all the hills moved lightly. I beheld, and, lo, there was no man, and all the birds of the heavens were fled. I beheld, and, lo, the fruitful place was a wilderness, and all the cities thereof were broken down at the presence of the Lord, and by his fierce anger" [Jeremiah 4:23-26].

Now turn to Jeremiah 25:33: "And the slain of the Lord shall be at that day from one end of the earth even unto the other end of the earth: they shall not be lamented, neither gathered, nor buried."

Sunlight: I would surely hate to pace around in such a desolate spot for a thousand years awaiting my doom. To say nothing of trying to quiet an uneasy conscience.

Joe: I doubt he has a conscience anymore. But let's wind up this story with the great, breathtaking finale.

Carol: May I tell it, Pastor Joe? I don't know the texts, but I know the story.

Joe: Fire away, Button.

Carol: Well, when the thousand years are finished—imagine a thousand years in heaven—then the beautiful city of God in which we've lived comes back to this earth [Revelation 21:2]. But remember the verse that said the wicked lived not again until the thousand years were finished? Well, when they are raised, Satan thinks he can conquer God's people with such a vast army [Revelation 20:7, 8] so he gets them organized for battle and marches up against the holy city, but the Bible says that "fire came down from God out of heaven, and devoured them" [verse 9]. And that's the end of sin forever.

Sunlight: You know, we always think of the Second Coming as the end, but in reality it's only the beginning!

Michael: Let's read Revelation 21 together before we turn in. Somehow it comforts me to think we will come back to this earth one day, and even though it's made over new and infinitely more beautiful [Revelation 21:1, 5], I guess I have a secret hope that we will recognize a familiar spot here and there. Sometimes these very mountains in which we live seem so beautiful one wonders how our Lord will improve upon them, but I presume He has wonders that my meager mind has never dreamed of [1 Corinthians

2:9].

How clearly my new friends have charted the course ahead of them. It is sad that all the world has not searched the Book as they have. Only a moment of time remains, and well it is, for the fear and suffering on Planet Earth have risen to heartbreaking proportions.

The early months of winter lock the group into their mountain retreat with persistent snows. They live together in a sweet harmony of spirit, rare under such conditions. Survival occupies most of their time, and the rest they spend in prayer and study, interspersed with hiking and play in the out-of-doors with the children. There is ever a sense of waiting and of concern for their loved ones from whom they are separated. Food and heat are both scarce and must be rationed, creating continual discomfort.

On a cold, clear night with a silver moon spangling the mountaintops, eight snowmobiles shatter the stillness and startle Meg and her friends from a deep and peaceful sleep. Joe and Michael slip into robes and cross the frosty floors to open the door. Ten state policemen stand upon their doorstep. The two men know the quick fear that has become familiar to thousands of their fellow Christians around the world. Joe invites them inside, and Michael lights the oil lamp in the middle of the table. The other members of the group move quietly into the room.

Police Officer *(glancing around at them):*   How long have you people been living here?

Joe: This is our second winter.

Police Officer: Why are you here?

Joe: We prefer this simple life to the dangers and health hazards of the city.

Police Officer *(irritation growing in his voice and showing on his face):*   How did you acquire this property?

Michael: My father gave it to me. He summered here for many years.

(Another policeman angrily motions the first one aside.)

Police Officer 2: What religion do you belong to?

Joe: We are followers of Jesus Christ and trust in His blood for our salvation.

Police Officer: Never mind that. What day do you worship on?

Joe *(hesitating only a moment):* The seventh—Saturday.

Police Officer *(smiling strangely):* Is there a child here named Carol?

Joe: Yes, there is.

Police Officer: She is under our protection at the request of our informant. The rest of you will be shot at six in the morning when the law goes into effect.

Joe: What law?

Police Officer *(scowling):* I find it hard to believe you're unaware of the events taking place in the world. Surely you know that all who disregard the sacredness of Sunday and stubbornly refuse to honor that day will be killed.

Joe: I knew that such a law was in the offing, but it is hard to accept the fact that freedom-loving Americans would allow such an edict. What charge has been brought against us?

Police Officer: That you have invited disaster upon our world by your persistent refusal to recognize the sacredness of Sunday. You have angered God, and we will have peace only when the earth is rid of the likes of you.

Joe: Are these your personal convictions or those of the state?

Police Officer: I didn't come here to be interrogated. *I* will ask the questions. *(He gestures at Dale.)* Young man, build up the fire, and the rest of you sit down in a circle about the fireplace and say what you will to each other and—and your God, if you have one. You have only a few hours left.

Where is the child Carol?

Carol: Right here, sir.

Officer: Don't worry. You'll return with us and be placed in your father's care.

Carol: Was it my father who told you we were here?

Officer: Young lady, I said *I* will ask the questions. But *(chuckling)* I guess it doesn't make much difference one way or the other at this point. No, it was not your father. It was a man named Bill Norris.

Sunlight *(quietly to Michael):* Sybil must have hated that. I'm thankful Carol can go free. Darling, do you think we're ready to die?

Michael: Only—only through the blood of Jesus, Maggie. Thank God we accepted it long ago as our preparation for this moment.

Joe: Let us sing, my people. We have come to the end of our long vigil here in the mountains. Though we have been cold and hungry, it has been a sweet and sacred time. Death is not to be feared. It is only a short detour on the way to the kingdom. It is a privilege to join the Lord in suffering. How about "When I Survey the Wondrous Cross"?

(As the singing fills the room Carol speaks softly to her mother.)

Carol: They aren't really going to shoot everyone, are they?

Sunlight: I fear they really mean it, but don't be afraid, Love. Daddy and Marie will take good care of you. Jesus will come soon, and we can all be together again just as we've planned. Tell Sybil that we died happy and full of hope. Tell her, Baby, that I loved her and owe everything to her.

Carol: I would rather just stay here. I'm not afraid to die.

Sunlight: I don't think you have any choice. Remember

when Michael and I are gone that Jesus is always with you.
I love you, Sweetheart. You have been a great comfort to
Michael and to me these hard months. You're a good little
soldier of the cross. Now let's sing with the others.

   *(Meg holds Carol close against her and finds she
cannot join in the singing for the lump in her throat.)*
Combined voices:

> "There is a happy land
>   Far, far away,
> Where saints in glory stand,
>   Bright, bright as day.
> O! how they sweetly sing,
> 'Worthy is our Saviour King';
> Loud let His praises ring,
>   Praise, praise for aye."

   *(Over the singing comes another sound, loud, un-
natural, and frightening. Beneath the old house the
ground heaves and shudders. Both singers and police
race from the building in terror. Outside they find the
skies overcast with an eerie blackness, while ear-
shattering thunder rolls over the earth. Vivid gashes of
lightning splinter the darkness [Revelation 16:18].)*

Jason: Dad, the mountains are moving—they really are.
Everything is moving. We will never survive.

Joe *(tears streaming down his face):*   Son, this is not a time
to fear. It is a time to rejoice.

Jason: You mean this is it? Jesus is coming?

   *(He looks about him and sees Sunlight, Michael,
and the others kneeling upon the quivering earth, their
faces lifted upward, radiant with joy. Following their
gaze, he finds the softest, most delicate rainbow span-
ning the angry heavens and hears a voice speaking the*

*words, "I will that they also, whom thou hast given me,
be with me where I am" [John 17:24].)*

All about the kneeling company fall great hailstones [Revelation 16:21], but none touch them. The wind shrieks and moans with hurricane intensity, flattening their clothing against their bodies, splintering trees to the earth. Lightning hovers in sheets of flame. Those who had come to kill now huddle in terror among the boulders along the shore [Revelation 6:15-17].

Michael *(singing, and the others joining him):*   "God is our refuge and strength, a very present help in trouble. Therefore will not we fear, though the earth be removed, and though the mountains be carried into the midst of the sea; though the waters thereof roar and be troubled, though the mountains shake with the swelling thereof" [Psalm 46:1-3].

In the east a small cloud appears, growing larger and brighter as it comes nearer. Joe calls the attention of the rest to it, and they watch in fascination as it draws closer to the earth, its base a flame of fire, and above it the glorious rainbow that Jason had noted earlier. Beneath that rainbow sits enthroned the Prince of the universe.

Sunlight: Michael, it is happening. *It is really happening.* We're looking at Jesus. He is so beautiful. *(Tears of joy stream down her face.)*

Michael: I can't believe that this is real.

Carol: When will we see Jen, Mom?

Sunlight: Just wait, Darling. Don't miss a minute of this. We will see Jen. Never fear.

Carol: The lake has disappeared, Mother, and some of the mountains have collapsed. The earth looks like the landscape of the moon. It's a bottomless pit all right.

Sunlight glances about her in astonishment at the devastation. Could it have been only hours ago that she had stood for a moment on the front porch admiring the beauty of the mountains, snow, and moonlight? The voice of Jesus, melodic and powerful, rolls throughout the earth, calling the sleeping saints from their graves. From horizon to horizon the heavens seem filled with angels.

Joe *(reverently):* "Ten thousand times ten thousand, and thousands of angels."

Carol: Mom, look at Mr. Laird. He's not old anymore. He's young and strong like Michael. *(Her eyes grow big with astonishment.)* Mom, all your worry wrinkles are gone. You're beautiful [1 Corinthians 15:51, 52]!

Michael *(laughing and gathering her up in his arms):* That's just one of Jesus' gifts to us. Just the beginning, Sweetheart.

Tammie: Look, there are thousands of people being drawn up toward Jesus. *(Even as she speaks, the little group themselves move heavenward, angels at their side.)*

Carol: Mom, oh, Mom, an angel is bringing Jen. She sees us. She's letting go of the angel's hand. She's coming. Oh, Mom, open up your arms.

   (Laughing and crying, Sunlight holds the form of her elder child tightly. Looking at Jesus, she whispers softly, "My Lord and my God, how can I ever thank You?" For a second His eyes meet hers, and she feels His love moving into and over her like small flames of joy.)

   The great fiery cloud hovers over the earth until the angels restore the last child to a mother's hungry arms, and then slowly, with its precious cargo of the saved, it lifts heavenward, alive with the sweet singing of a ransomed people, kneeling in adoration at the feet of the Prince.

   A tall and gentle angel takes his place beside Sunlight. "I want to give you a very special welcome to your new life," *he says.* "My name is Jared."

GOD WANTS YOU TO ENJOY A FULL ABUNDANT, HAPPY LIFE, RIGHT HERE! RIGHT NOW!

Which is why the FOCUS ON LIVING series of Bible study guides was prepared—to introduce you to all the wonderful things God wants you to have.

In FOCUS ON LIVING you'll find out how to make your home a happier place. You'll find out how to make your life happier than you ever thought possible. And you'll find out the whys behind unhappy things like war, suffering, and death.

The eleven-lesson set is free. Simply fill out and return the coupon below, or send your name and address on a postcard requesting the FOCUS ON LIVING study guides.

Get your life into focus with FOCUS ON LIVING. Do it today.

- -

Please send me the free FOCUS ON LIVING series of Bible study guides. I understand there is no cost or obligation. (Offer good only in the United States and Canada. Please do not order course for anyone other than yourself.)

Name _____
(Please print.)

Address _____

City _____ State_____ Zip_____

Send coupon to:
FOCUS ON LIVING
P.O. Box 55
Los Angeles, California 90053